CAPTIVATED BY
THE BROODING
BILLIONAIRE

CAPTIVATED BY THE BROODING BILLIONAIRE

REBECCA WINTERS

MILLS & BOON

First published in Great Britain 2018
by Mills & Boon, an imprint of HarperCollins*Publishers*
1 London Bridge Street, London, SE1 9GF

Large Print edition 2018

© 2018 Rebecca Winters

ISBN: 978-0-263-07405-5

MIX
Paper from
responsible sources
FSC® C007454

This book is produced from independently certified
FSC™ paper to ensure responsible forest management.
For more information visit www.harpercollins.co.uk/green.

Printed and bound in Great Britain
by CPI Group (UK) Ltd, Croydon, CR0 4YY

To my beloved, generous, marvellous
parents, who let their teenage daughter
attend school in Switzerland, where
a whole world opened up to her that
she'd never dreamed about or imagined.
To have been born to such
wonderful parents is my greatest blessing.

PROLOGUE

"Nigel?"

A tap on the opened office door caused Abby Grant to look up from the desk. During this year's summer and fall semesters at San José State University in California, she and Nigel, the visiting professor from Cambridge, England, had offices in the same literature department. They'd fallen in love and often worked side by side in one office or the other while they planned a spring wedding.

"Dr. Belmont is teaching his final class before Christmas break," she said to the thirtyish brunette woman dressed in a suit. Maybe she was a student, but Abby didn't recognize her. "He should be finished at noon. I'm Ms. Grant, one of the teachers in the department. Would you like to leave a message for him with me? I'll make sure he gets it."

"That won't be necessary," the woman said in a British accent as strong as Nigel's. He'd let Abby know right away he spoke an "estuary" dialect. "I'm Lucy Belmont, Nigel's wife. I need to speak to him in person, so I'll wait in here until he returns."

Abby blinked in surprise. "I'm afraid you've come to the wrong place. The Nigel Belmont who's a visiting professor here doesn't have a wife."

A tight smile broke out on Lucy Belmont's face. "Indeed he does and two children. They're expecting a visit from him over Christmas. Here are some pictures taken last spring."

The woman handed a packet to Abby, who opened it and saw Nigel in photo after photo with this woman and two children.

Abby took the packet with shaking hands. Was this some kind of a joke? Could this woman be a sister-in-law or even a sister Abby had never heard of? Or was she a woman who had some pathetic attachment to Nigel? None of this made sense. Abby and Nigel were planning their wedding!

Not wanting to get into anything unpleasant with Lucy until she'd talked to Nigel, Abby got up from the desk. "I had no idea. Of course, you're welcome to stay here. He should be back in about fifteen minutes. If you'll excuse me."

With her heart racing, Abby left the room and hurried down the hallway to the stairs. The lecture theaters were one story below. She slipped inside the room of thirty plus students and sat down at the back while she waited for Nigel to finish up his lecture.

He was popular with the students and looked the part of the jaunty professor in his tweed jacket with his dark blond hair brushed back.

She knew he had spotted her, but he continued talking and finally excused his students so they could enjoy the holiday.

When the last one left the room, Nigel gathered up his briefcase and walked toward her, giving her a quick kiss on her lips. "To what do I owe this unexpected visit from my beautiful fiancée?"

Abby stared hard at him, not wanting to believe what she was thinking. "There's a woman waiting for you in your office who says she's your wife. She introduced herself as Lucy Belmont and showed me pictures of her with you and two children. Please tell me this is a joke." Her throbbing voice reverberated in the room.

Nigel didn't move a muscle, but the light faded from his eyes. The change was enough to tell her the other woman had been speaking the truth. Pain almost incapacitated her. She backed away from him. "So she *is* your wife!"

He shook his head. "Look, Abby. It's a long story. We've been separated close to a year. The divorce will be final soon. You have to listen to me. I would have eventually told you, but—"

"What kind of a man are you?" she broke in on him, destroyed by his admission. "To think we've been together all this time and a whole other part of your life has been a huge secret—"

In a flash, the happy world Abby had inhabited had disintegrated.

You've been in love with a cunning, monstrous, devious cheat!

Abby had often heard the expression about blood draining from a person's face. She knew that was happening to her now and feared she would be sick right in front of him. Besides betraying her and his spouse, how many other women had he deceived? Those poor children.

She took off the engagement ring and flung it at him before dashing out of the room to the hallway. The second she reached the restroom, she retched until nothing more came up.

When she was able to stand without holding on to the sink, she hurried upstairs to her own office for her purse and left the campus. In her pain she needed to talk to the people she trusted and loved. Instead of driving to her apartment near the campus, she headed for her parents' home in San José.

* * *

Abby stayed with her parents for several days, after which she talked with Dr. Stewart, the head of her department, about her situation. Once she'd told Dr. Stewart the truth, Abby asked if she could have a leave of absence for the next semester.

To her great relief she was granted a leave and also offered an opportunity to do some research abroad in Europe until the summer. After experiencing a world of pain, nothing could have suited her better than to get away. Best of all, she was assured that Dr. Belmont would no longer be on the staff at San José State and would be teaching at a college back east. She would never have to see him again.

After Christmas, Abby flew to LA for a week's worth of meetings to collaborate with two other women on the project before going overseas. Ginger Lawrence and Zoe Perkins, who both had similar literature backgrounds from Stanford and UCLA respectively, had also been hired. The three of them, close in age, bonded fast. The thought of going to Europe with the girls gave Abby something to look forward to and the courage to make some changes in her life. So, before returning to San José to pack and leave for Europe with them, Abby decided to get a makeover and visited a beauty salon.

The lady in charge told her to be seated. While Abby waited, she poured through some magazines. In a few minutes one of the hairdressers beckoned her over to the chair. Abby took the magazine with her.

"What can I do for you?"

"I'd like you to cut and style my hair like *this*!" She showed her the picture she liked most. It was a bouncy bob with graduated layers. Each curled layer ending somewhere between the chin and the shoulders. She wanted something in between.

"Are you sure? All this long gold hair cut off?" The hairdresser acted shocked, as if Abby had asked for something sinful. How funny. Why did this woman care what she wanted?

Three weeks ago Abby had cut Nigel Belmont out of her life so fast, he hadn't seen it coming. After Christmas he'd tried to talk to her once on the phone and she'd told him to go to hell in so many words. She'd meant it and it had felt good!

Cutting her hair was her last act to separate herself from any semblance to the old Abby— she'd since vowed never to be duped by a man again.

The woman shook her head, but she did as Abby asked. An hour later she almost squealed in delight after looking in the mirror. Abby hardly recognized herself. Her apple-green eyes appeared larger and she thought she actually looked her age of twenty-six instead of the tired-looking thirty she'd seemed to be. She'd needed something simple and easy. That was the whole idea!

Abby paid the woman a nice tip. Before leaving the salon, she had to tiptoe over her long locks of silvery-blond hair but did it with no regrets.

CHAPTER ONE

Five months later

WITH HER LAPTOP packed between the sweaters in her suitcase, Abby left the bedsitter in Cologny, Switzerland, where she'd been staying for the last two weeks, and took a taxi to the train station in Geneva, Switzerland.

With her massive research project finished, today marked the first day of her vacation. No longer restricted to suits and dresses, Abby had pulled on her favorite pair of jeans and a crew neck, short sleeve white-on-black print blouse. She had the whole month of June to have fun before returning to San José.

Abby couldn't wait to be with her friends again. They'd Skyped and phoned each other—sent emails—but it would be great to do things together in person.

Once in graduate school she'd become a teaching assistant in the humanities department and had worked hard. Specializing in the romance writers of the early nineteenth century, she'd received her doctorate, after which she'd been given more classes to teach. That's when she'd met Nigel. In hindsight, what a disaster that meeting had turned out to be!

But she'd learned she wasn't the only one who'd been burned in a relationship. One of the girls, Zoe, had just come out of a bitter divorce because her husband had been unfaithful. She'd insisted she would never want anything to do with a man again. Abby didn't need to get inside Zoe's skin to understand how she felt.

The pain of putting your trust in the man you loved only to discover he hadn't loved you or believed in the sanctity of marriage had been too devastating. Abby felt like her heart had been murdered. How could she ever trust anyone again?

As for Ginger, she'd lost her husband recently to cancer and needed to get away from the pain.

In a short time the three of them had developed a special camaraderie, and all three of them were ready to play.

Being in an especially good mood, Abby gave the driver a nice tip and walked inside the train station with her suitcase. Since she had fifteen minutes before she needed to board her train, she headed directly for her favorite food kiosk. She'd eaten here every time she'd needed to take the train someplace.

After making her selection of six small quiches, two for herself and two for each her friends, she bought a second-class ticket and boarded the crowded train.

She found a compartment and sat down across from a priest and a couple of teenagers speaking German. They started to listen to rock music, but their earphones didn't block the sound all that much. Abby didn't mind. Not so the priest, who finally got up and left the compartment. She decided she would wait to eat until she met the girls at the village of St.

Saphorin, an hour and a half or so and a quick change of trains away.

The quiet, efficient train ran alongside Lake Geneva, the famous croissant-shaped lake called lac Léman by the locals. Abby settled back, almost preening like a cat in the sun because she was so happy to be free of responsibilities. The train glided from one picturesque village to another in a gentle rhythm.

The surroundings that included the sapphire-blue lake with the snow-crested French Alps in the distance mesmerized her. Before long she had to change trains and it wasn't long after that that St. Saphorin appeared, wedged between the water and terraced rows of vineyards that ran up the steep hillsides.

When the train came to a stop, she reached for her suitcase and left the compartment. Several other passengers had already descended. Finally, she was going to see her friends. Abby was eager to be with them and on vacation.

Yesterday Zoe had flown to Venice, Italy, from Athens, Greece, to meet up with Ginger who'd been doing research in Italy. The two of them had boarded the night train to Switzerland. They'd planned to get off in Montreux to pick up the rental car and drive the few kilometers to St. Saphorin.

Relieved to be here, Abby walked around to the front of the station. There was no sign of the girls yet. She sat down and took in the sight of the Jura Mountains in the distance while she waited. After twenty minutes, she phoned Ginger and had to leave a message. Then she called Zoe, who answered.

"Abby? Are you in St. Saphorin?"

"Yes. Where are you?"

"The rental car we were promised isn't ready yet. Too many tourists were booked. Ginger is dealing with them now. It may be a while, so I phoned the château where we'll be staying. Someone will come for you soon. I gave them a description of you. Just stay put. We can't wait to see you!"

"Same here," Abby said before hanging up.

Someone was coming to get her, but it could

be a while. She reached for a quiche and savored every bite. In the distance, she took in the vision of gray stone walls and steep inclines covered by the famous Lavaux vineyards of the region. They were riddled with hiking trails, a sport the Swiss adored. So, did Abby. She loved the yellowish colors of the homes spotting the landscape.

How lucky she and the girls were to be the recipients of their boss's largesse! Magda Collier, one of the most acclaimed female film directors in Hollywood had hired the three of them to do research for a movie being produced by a revered mogul friend of hers.

After the New Year, Magda had brought Abby and the girls together in Los Angeles for a week with some writers who were working on an important script. She wanted to create a historically authentic film that accentuated the positive aspects of the colorful life of Lord Byron, the famous British romantic poet and satirist.

They'd been thrilled about the project and had become friends.

Magda had assigned each of them a different area in Europe to do research, and Abby had been sent to Switzerland. Now, because of their "great work"—Magda's words after they'd turned in their information—she'd delighted them with a reward. It turned out to be a vacation at a château and vineyard called the Clos de la Floraison on the shores of Lake Geneva. Nothing could have pleased them more.

Magda explained she had a permanent arrangement with the old owner of the vineyard. From time to time she used it for herself and guests to enjoy. They could stay there while they did all the touring they wanted around the region.

Since the three of them had to return to their teaching assignments for the upcoming fall semester, they planned to take advantage of this time together and sightsee to their hearts' content.

As they had another month before going back to the US, Abby was also hoping to find evidence of a poem that Lord Byron had been rumored to write called *Labyrinths*, or some such title, while he'd been in Switzerland. But it was a work that had never seen the light of day and many experts dismissed it as sheer fiction. But Abby hadn't given up on the possibility of finding out the truth, if it existed.

Recently a fragment of a memoir by Claire Clairmont, who'd traveled in Switzerland with Byron, had been found in a branch of New York public library. It had shed new light on Lord Byron and Shelley. What Abby would give to unearth a find equally sensational, but no amount of digging had been successful so far.

While Abby sat there beneath a sunny sky, wondering where else she and the girls might look while they were here for the month, she noticed a vintage black Renault drive up and park.

Out stepped a tall man, maybe early thirties, who stood fit and lean. With his overly long black wavy hair, he epitomized her idea of the quintessential drop-dead sensational male. She didn't know such a person existed.

Only a Frenchman had that appeal, the kind

she'd conjured in her mind and fantasized about from time to time growing up. He had an expression much like the one she'd seen on the French actor Charles Boyer who had played the lead in a famous old film classic *The Garden of Allah*.

Abby had been a teenager when she'd first watched it and had fallen in love with the actor. He played the part of a monk who ran away from a monastery in North Africa and fell in love with an Englishwoman. They went out in the desert together, but he carried a terrible secret.

At times his sadness combined with his male beauty was almost painful to watch. Abby had watched it over and over again. His performance had seemed so real that she always been haunted by him and had decided there was no Frenchman alive more captivating.

Until now.

Abby couldn't take her eyes off the stranger, something that had never happened to her before, not with Nigel or the boyfriend she'd loved earlier in her life. There was a brooding aura about him that caught at her emotions though she fought not to be attracted.

Who was he? Where had such a man come from?

Abby felt as if he was burdened by a great weight. It was there in the way he carried himself. The lines radiating from his eyes and around his mouth spelled pain. His work clothes, a white shirt with the sleeves shoved up to the elbows and dark trousers, told her he'd stopped whatever he'd been doing to get in his car and drive here.

This was the magnificent someone who'd come for her?

His bronzed complexion, close to a teak color, overlay chiseled features. The man worked in the sun. Beneath black brows his midnight-black eyes met hers and roved over her with an intensity that sent a ripple of sensation through her. She trembled for no good reason, something she couldn't prevent.

There was an unrehearsed sensuality about

the way his hard mouth smiled almost derisively, as if he knew she'd shivered slightly and found it amusing. Even though he'd caught her staring, she refused to avert her eyes. Her pulse raced as he approached her.

"Mademoiselle Grant?"

Those two words, spoken in a deep seductive voice, curled their way through to her insides. She heard no trace of the singsong French spoken in this part of Switzerland. He was a Frenchman down to every atom of his hard-muscled body.

"Yes. You must be from La Floraison."

He nodded. "I was told to look for a woman with golden hair." His excellent, heavily accented English came as a shock.

"You have the advantage. They didn't tell me your name."

"Raoul Decorvet."

"I thought Magda's friend was a great deal older."

"He was. Sadly, Auguste died a month ago at the age of eighty."

"Oh, no—" she cried. "We didn't know. Magda didn't tell us."

"You weren't supposed to know."

Abby shook her head. "I don't understand."

"I'm here negotiating the sale of this property business for the former owner. Auguste had a bad heart so he never knew how long he had to live. The vineyard managers, Louis and Gabrielle, have said that you and your friends are welcome to stay here for the month. I was on hand when Gabrielle received a distress call from your friends. She was busy so I offered my help."

"Thank you, but this isn't right. We don't want to put anyone out."

Again, she felt his penetrating gaze wander over her, missing nothing before it rested on her hair. "It's no imposition. If you'll get in the car, I'll explain while I drive you to the château."

His potent male charisma made her so aware of him, it was hard to act natural. She felt nervous. After her experience with Nigel, Abby was almost frightened by her visceral response to this total stranger who blew away every man she'd ever known. He reached for her suitcase and helped her into the front passenger seat before putting it in the back.

After he'd started the car, she said, "I'm sorry you had to come for me. I could have waited until my friends showed up. Providing taxi service is hardly the work of a busy Realtor."

"Pas de problème."

Abby was sure that wasn't true, but Raoul Decorvet had a certain air of authority. She didn't want to argue with him since he'd put himself out on her behalf, so she kept quiet while he started the car. They headed toward the road and wound around the village toward the hillside. En route she detected a flowery scent.

"What is that fragrance I can smell in the air?"

"La Floraison is greeting you."

She studied his striking profile. "What do you mean?"

"The flowers of the grape vines open in June.

This is the reason why Magda wanted you to come now. For the next fifteen days, they'll emit their intoxicating perfume while they undergo automatic pollination. Their dual reproductive organs, mostly female among the male, ensure the future of the species." Their glances fused. "Nature's way is remarkable, *n'est-ce pas*?"

For some reason the subject of their conversation sounded personal, especially the way he said it in that deep, silky voice. It brought heat to Abby's cheeks. "Have you found a buyer yet?" she asked in order to change the subject, hoping to break his spell over her.

"*Oui*. It's already done. The new owner will take possession at the end of June."

"Please don't tell me you put it off for the benefit of me and my friends."

"For your information, it's to honor the commitment Auguste made. While you're here, Gabrielle will take care of you. You'll be staying in the unattached farmhouse next to the château and should be comfortable there."

"I'm sure it will be wonderful." Magda had

seen to that, but the appearance of this fascinating Frenchman had knocked the foundations out from under her.

Before long the château came into view. Abby marveled at the gray stone structure. It reminded her of a small fortress and caught at her imagination. In former times it would have been a commanding landmark.

He drove them along rows of lush vineyards in full flower and past a thriving vegetable garden until they arrived at a charming farmhouse with a mansard roof.

"There's Gabrielle now. It's getting late in the day. She'll make something for you to eat if you're hungry."

"No, no. I'll wait for my friends."

Abby spotted the wiry, middle-aged woman wearing a straw hat with a broad rim, who came around the side of the farmhouse. She was dressed in slacks and a tunic.

"Bonjour!"

The woman's warm smile made Abby feel

welcome. She got out of the car, liking her already. *"Bonjour, Madame."*

"Soyez la bienvenue!"

"Merci. Thank you."

"I see Raoul found you." The Swiss people impressed her with their ability to speak good English. "My husband is up in the higher vineyard and I was doing some pruning. When your friends called about their difficulty, Raoul volunteered to take our car and go for you."

"I'm very grateful to both of you."

"I understand they should be here soon. Come inside with me." She reached for Abby's suitcase. "We have five bedrooms with en suite bathrooms. Since you are the first one to arrive, you may have your pick."

"This is exciting. I've been looking forward to this vacation for a long time."

Abby turned to Raoul. He was too gorgeous and too intriguing. She should be relieved to say goodbye to him, yet deep down she would rather have stayed outside to talk to him, which was crazy. He had the power to sweep any woman away, especially Abby. She couldn't believe her feelings were so strong, not when she'd promised herself never to get seriously involved with any man for the rest of her life.

"Thank you for picking me up."

His brooding dark eyes narrowed on her features. Again, she sensed he was in some kind of turmoil. She could feel it. "Don't forget this." He handed her the purse she'd left in the car.

What on earth was wrong with her? In his company she'd forgotten all about it and had left it lying on the seat. The slight contact of skin against skin sent another shiver through her body. *"À bientôt, mademoiselle."*

She knew that phrase well enough. It meant "see you soon." To read any real meaning into it meant she was a fool. But he *had* called her *mademoiselle*. Maybe he'd noticed she wore no rings. For that matter she hadn't seen a wedding ring on his finger either, but that didn't necessarily mean he wasn't married.

Abby turned and followed Gabrielle inside the house, but her mind was filled with unanswered questions about him. Why would a French Realtor be doing business here?

Maybe he lived on the French side of Lac Léman and was authorized to operate in both countries. In that case he wouldn't be staying at the château. If he had a car, where was it? She wondered if he'd be leaving soon. The manager would know the answers, but if Abby were to ask her anything, it would suggest she was interested.

Don't do this, Abby. Don't be a fool.

Gabrielle led her through the beamed common rooms. She found the restored nineteenth-century farmhouse warm and inviting. They went upstairs to the bedrooms. Each had a mini fridge filled with drinks, and every room had a basket filled with fruit and Swiss chocolate.

Abby chose a room that looked out over the vineyard to the west. She could see the estate workers. One of them was probably Louis. Of course there was no sign of Raoul.

"If you need anything, pick up the bedside phone and ring the château. I'll answer. Your friends know to come straight to the farmhouse. Your breakfast will be laid out at seven every morning in the dining room."

Abby turned to Gabrielle. "Everything is perfect. Will it be all right to open the window? I love the fragrance coming from the vineyard."

"Of course."

"Thank you."

"De rien. À tout à l'heure, mademoiselle."

CHAPTER TWO

AFTER GABRIELLE LEFT, Abby undid the lever and pushed the window open. The smell was divine. She unpacked her suitcase. With that done she put her purse and laptop on a round table in the corner around which several uphol- stered chairs had been arranged.

The bathroom contained every amenity. Once she'd refreshed herself and put on her frosted tangerine-colored lipstick, she went downstairs and walked outside.

There was no point in lying to herself. While Abby waited for the girls, she felt compelled to see Raoul again and couldn't understand it. What was it about him? How could he create all these feelings and yearnings roiling inside of her in one short meeting?

Again, she had to question her sanity after

what she'd experienced with Nigel. But she'd never felt like this with him. Not even close. Their attraction had grown over time with mutual interests.

Nothing could match this violent explosion of feelings that had made her heart trip over itself from the moment Raoul got out of the old Renault and walked toward her. The Frenchman had caused her to forget the lesson she'd thought she'd learned following Nigel's treachery.

Something was definitely wrong with her. It scared her that she was so drawn to him. Afraid of her feelings, Abby ran back toward the farmhouse and waited in front to watch for her friends.

She checked her watch. Since boarding the train, time had gotten away from her. It said 5:00 p.m. Concerned at this point, she pulled out her cell to call them. But just then she saw a dark red car pull up. She put the phone away and ran toward them.

"You're here at last!"

Her friends got out and both hugged Abby. Zoe smiled at her. "You look great!"

"So you do you guys."

"Sorry we're so late, but nothing's perfect."

"It doesn't matter. I'm thankful we're all here in one piece."

"Obviously you were picked up at the station."

An image of Raoul flashed through her mind, causing her body to melt like butter in the sun. "Their Realtor picked me up."

Ginger eyed her. "What Realtor is that?"

"Why don't we drive to the cheese fondue restaurant Magda told us about and I'll tell you everything. But first let's get you settled."

When the girls heard the news about Auguste, they would feel as sad as she had. Abby decided that it would be better to prolong their happiness by eating first. "Sounds great."

The three of them hugged again. She helped carry their things inside and led them up the stairs. "You have your choice of four rooms."

Zoe entered a room with an antique armoire and declared it her home away from home. Her dark blond hair worn in a windblown style had new highlights streaked by the sun while she'd been in Greece. With her azure blue eyes she was a knockout.

Abby's friends were both attractive. Ginger's gray eyes combined with her cap of black curls made her look French. She could be taken for a movie star. They inspected the other three rooms and she chose one that looked out on the lake. After opening her window, Ginger turned to them.

"I'm starving, you guys. We had to wait forever for the car. I say we unpack later and go eat!"

"You won't get an argument out of me." Abby ran to her bedroom for her purse and hurried outside with the girls.

Since Ginger had done the negotiating, she was the designated driver. That was fine with Abby who kept her eyes glued for any sign of Raoul, but he didn't make an appearance. She should be thankful, not crushed that she might never see him again.

Determined to put him out of her mind, she sat back, resigned to enjoy the bucolic scenery. But that was easier said than done. Raoul's image wouldn't leave her mind.

Zoe served as navigator and pulled the directions Magda had given them out of her purse. "We have to drive to the small village of Chexbres, which according to Magda is seven hundred feet above the lake. We should pass through the most important Swiss wine region. Apparently their main product is a table grape wine."

"The Swiss call it *chasselas*," Abby added her two cents. She loved the sound of the word. "I've learned a lot about it while I've been working here."

They drove higher, gasping over the landscape. "You guys—" Ginger cried out. "Look at those rows of grape vines going up that steep hill! It's amazing!"

"That's why they have to be terraced," Abby explained. "Sometimes they use pulleys and have to be irrigated because the Rhône valley can get warm and dry here."

Zoe had opened her window. "I love this climate. Smell that air. Delicious."

Her comment reminded Abby of those moments with Raoul when he'd told her about the fragrance from the flowers at La Floraison. Nature truly was remarkable to have created a man like him, but she kept that memory to herself.

They continued to drive until they reached the town of Chexbres with its magnificent view. "There it is! The Lion d'Or." Ginger pulled over to the curb near the restaurant and they went inside for a feast of cheese fondue eaten with French bread.

Their hunger was at a pitch and they ate every morsel of bread accompanied by goblets of *chasselas*.

"Before we plan what we're going to do tomorrow, tell us about this Realtor who picked you up. You've been kind of quiet about that."

Abby looked at Zoe. The time had come. "I have something important to tell you guys. It came as a shock to me."

"What?" Ginger asked.

"Magda's friend Auguste, the owner of the château, died last month."

Both girls fell back into their seats. "What?"

"I think the man who came to get me must be a Realtor because he's been here selling the estate. His name is Raoul Decorvet. We've been allowed to stay on until the end of June when the new owner takes possession. It's Magda's wish."

Ginger frowned. "You're kidding! She never said anything. We can't go on living here now. It wouldn't be right." Zoe shook her head in agreement.

Abby knew that would be the girls' reaction. "I feel the same way. Since we're in Europe, where would you guys like to go? I need to conserve my funds, but I've been budgeting in my mind. I believe I have enough money to spend two weeks here. What about you two?"

They both figured two weeks would be all they could afford.

"Any ideas where you'd like to go?"

Zoe took a deep breath. "If I had the chance, I'd fly back to Greece in a minute."

That didn't surprise Abby. Their divorced friend hadn't said anything, but Abby sensed there was a man involved. "What part exactly?"

"Patras. I didn't get to spend nearly enough time in that area."

"Maybe we could take a small tour of some of the Greek Islands too. What do you think, Ginger?"

"Not that I wouldn't love to travel there, but to be honest, I'd rather go back to Italy. There's so much to see and it's so glorious. I couldn't get enough of it." By the tone in her voice, Abby wondered if Ginger had also experienced some kind of romantic interest.

As for Abby, she'd met a mysterious Frenchman earlier today, but it was best she never saw him again. "Where do you want to visit in Italy, Ginger?"

"Venice. It's the most romantic city on earth."

Well, well. Their friend *did* have a reason to want to go back. Abby was sure of it.

"I have an idea. If we pool our resources, we can afford a two-week vacation. Maybe we could drive to Venice tomorrow and spend a few days there before visiting Rome. From there we'll fly to Patras and tour around that area for a week before we go back to California. What do you think?"

Ginger looked at Zoe before she said, "What do *you* want to do, Abby?"

She wanted to stay longer and see if she could find that rumored poem, but it probably didn't exist. "I've been living in Switzerland since January and am ready for a new adventure." Which was true.

"Not even one guy has caught your eye who wants you to hang around?"

Zoe had just given herself away.

Abby shook her head. "I'm not ready to meet a man."

Ginger's eyebrows shot up. "You will be when the right one comes along."

Someone out of this world *had* come along earlier today, but she needed to run from him and keep running. "Let's change the subject. Are you guys on board with our plans?"

"According to Magda, we have to visit the Maison Cailler Chocolate Factory in Broc," Zoe interjected. "She has already paid for us to take the tour. Why don't we at least do that tomorrow to make her happy?"

Abby eyed them both. "I toured that plant in March. It's really worth the time. While you do that, I'd like to do a little more research on Byron while we're in St. Saphorin.

"Maybe you guys should drop me off at the local library in the village. That's one place I haven't visited. Then I'll walk back to the farmhouse and wait for you. If you two leave in the morning, you'll be back by afternoon and we can leave for Italy." Magda was funding their rental car.

They agreed it was a great idea and drove back to the château. If Raoul Decorvet was still around in the morning, Abby didn't plan to be here. She would be insane to hope they might see each other again. She had the fear that getting involved with a man who made her feel this besotted without even knowing him could destroy her.

After a shower and shave, Raoul Capet Regnac Decorvet, the elder son of the duke of the Vosne-Romanée region in the Burgundy department of France, concluded his business with the new owner of La Floraison.

Once Raoul had assured him he'd be back at the end of June to tie up any loose ends, he hung up the phone and ate the breakfast Gabrielle had brought to his room in the château. He drank more coffee and made half a dozen calls to members of his staff while he looked down from the upstairs window that faced the courtyard.

The three women had left early in their rental car and hadn't returned. He knew from Gabrielle they hadn't checked out. To his shock, Mademoiselle Grant hadn't left his thoughts all night. He was overwhelmed by unfamiliar feelings for her that made him desperate to see her again. It astounded him he should have these desires when he'd only spent a few minutes with her. Nothing like this had ever happened to him in his life.

Raoul had of course enjoyed relationships with women from time to time growing up. It had been his destiny to marry the woman his father had demanded he marry, but he had felt nothing like this. Two years ago his wife and baby had tragically died in a car accident. Since then he'd been a slave to work.

When he came to Switzerland on business, he'd never dreamed he'd meet a woman who seemed to have invaded his mind, his psyche, his body the way she'd done yesterday. He couldn't explain it, but her effect on him had brought him alive.

His senses were involved from the moment he'd seen her sitting on the bench at the train station seemingly happy on her own. She'd made a breathtaking picture.

The sun's rays had turned her hair to liquid gold. Instead of wearing sunglasses like the typical tourist, she'd been drinking in the land-scape and had that look of a young woman on the brink of life.

He could feel her reacting to everything she saw. It made him breathless with excitement to observe her. She'd been in sync with his emotions when she'd wanted to know about that fragrance in the air. That aspect of her had fascinated him on a level that went deep beneath the surface.

There was a quality of innocence that appealed to him too. A gift like that wasn't present in the women who inhabited his world and certainly not within the confines of his own family. If innocence had been there once upon a time, their lifestyle and entitlements had robbed them of such an enticing virtue.

Why did he have to discover it now, with this woman who would be returning to the States shortly? She could never mean anything to him. Yet she already did mean something to him in a way that was so profound he couldn't let it go.

Lines darkened his Gallic features. They

would never cross paths again unless he made it happen. The longer he sat there, the stronger his resolve grew to see her again. He needed to explore these powerful feelings or lose his mind.

While he contemplated an idea that had been percolating in his brain all through the night, his cell rang. It was his private secretary getting back to him. He picked up.

"Félix?"

"You were right. Jules didn't think it was time yet, but he checked and said black rot *has* shown up in the *terroir* to the north."

"I knew it," Raoul murmured. "The weather has been warmer than usual. Even though I'll be home tomorrow, tell him to get started on the fungicide immediately. By now the infection is releasing spores."

"I'll get right on it."

"Don't let him put up an argument. The spray will stop this infection prior to the bloom period. Last year the spore production didn't happen this soon. I've told Jules all along this has to be checked every year due to weather changes. We may have to add an additional fungicide application after blooming occurs. Tell him I'll talk to him tomorrow."

Raoul hung up in time to see Mademoiselle Grant come walking up the drive. His pulse raced to realize she wasn't with her friends. He watched her pause at the vegetable garden to inspect some of the plants. She'd dressed in jeans and a short-sleeved green top, darker than her amazing eyes. On her feet she wore shoes for hiking.

He reached for his phone and keys, then left the room in jeans and a T-shirt to catch up with her before she disappeared. On his way out the door, he told Gabrielle he would inspect the château's powerboat to make sure it was in good shape for the new owner.

By the time he reached the outside, he glimpsed the younger woman walking along one of the vineyard paths beyond the vegetable garden. He strode toward her, admiring her shapely body as she paused to lean over and smell the flowers.

She must have sensed him coming and turned in his direction. Her gaze wandered over him as if she were startled to see him. "Hello. I had no idea you were still on the property. I guess I assumed you had real estate business elsewhere."

"I've only been here a few days. Tomorrow I'll be leaving for home."

"Does that mean you have a wife waiting for you?"

"No. I was married—" He hesitated, somehow knowing that he could confide in this beautiful stranger. "Tragically my wife and our baby died in a car crash two years ago. Angélique was coming home from her parents' château five kilometers away and was involved in an accident. The other driver was to blame."

Abby's eyes closed tightly. "I can't even imagine it." The brooding pain he exuded was no longer a mystery.

"Neither could I at the time, but it's in the past. What about your plans?"

"My friends and I will be leaving soon too. This morning they drove me into the village, then they went to tour the chocolate factory in Broc. I've already seen it and wanted to do some research. I expect they'll be back any minute now so I decided to stay out here and wait for them."

He frowned. "I thought I'd made it clear you're welcome to stay at La Floraison through the end of June."

"You did, but we talked about it and just don't feel it's right."

Raoul sucked in his breath. He knew she'd felt that way the moment he'd given her the news about Auguste. On reflection, he found it unusual that these women chose not to take advantage of the situation. Again, he found himself admiring her. "Does that mean you're flying back to the States?"

"Not yet. We're going to gallivant for two weeks in Italy and Greece. Then we'll go home."

"Not France?" He didn't want her to leave.

"I'd go there in a shot, but the girls have been

doing research in Italy and Greece since January. It's hard for them to leave, so they want to go back one last time now that they have the chance."

"What about you?"

"I've been working here in Switzerland."

He needed to know a lot more about her. "You've been here all this time?"

"Yes, but now I'm anxious for a change."

"Mademoiselle Grant," he began, "I have to take the château's boat out for a run on the lake to make sure it's in top order before I report to Louis. How would you like to go with me so we can continue our conversation? I'll drive us to the dock in their car."

"I'd better not. I can't swim."

Raoul could feel her pushing away from him, but in his gut he knew she wanted to go with him. There'd been an instant attraction between them.

"That's what life preservers are for. Can you imagine an accident happening in this giant bathtub of a lake? You can't even hear a lapping wave on the shore."

"You mean you think it's too placid?"

"Let's just say I can only take the peaceful ambience in doses."

"Our boss has led such a hectic life in Los Angeles, I can understand why she loves to come here every year to regenerate. She's a very generous woman to have offered us this vacation."

"I agree. Why don't you risk it and come with me? *I* can swim."

She looked hesitant. "I'd better not. I don't want to miss my friends."

Whatever was going on in her mind, he wasn't going to let her get away with it. "You have a phone."

"I know, but—"

"We wouldn't be gone long. I only need enough time to check out the engine and would like the company."

He heard her take a deep breath. "All right."

The chemistry between them was alive. She couldn't fight it any more than he could. If she'd said no, he would have been forced to come up with another ploy to spend time with her.

They started walking toward the Renault. He helped her into the car and drove them to the pier. The cabin cruiser was a few years old, but looked to be in good shape. Raoul walked along the dock and guided her into the boat. The first thing he did was hand her a life jacket.

"Thank you. What about you?"

Was she worried about him? He liked the idea of that. "If I need to, I'll grab one."

Raoul would have loved to help her put it on, but worried he wouldn't be able to restrain himself, he jumped back out to untie the ropes, then climbed in to start the engine. Once he'd backed out at a no-wake speed, he took off. Being with this woman was like a breath of fresh air.

She didn't have an agenda that prompted her to ask a lot of questions. He decided she was at peace with herself and seemed to enjoy the world around her. Raoul believed she was the kind of woman you could be with and not have to make conversation if you didn't want to.

"Why don't you sit opposite me?"

She sank down and glanced in the direction of the sailboats. "There's no wind. How sad they have to rely on motors."

Her comment was the same one he'd reflected on while being here. "Where have you been living in Switzerland?"

Abby eyed him curiously. "All over. Grindelwald, Lauterbrunnen, Mürren, Interlaken, Lake Thun, the Reichenbach and Staubbach Falls, Montreux, Geneva, Cologny."

"Why?"

"I guess you wouldn't know why our boss gave us this vacation."

"I only recall that she's a movie director in your country who was friends with Auguste."

"That's right. Magda is working on her most important film to date. It's a new look at the life of George Gordon Noel Byron, the Sixth Baron Byron, known as Lord Byron. She needs new eyes for fresh research to make the script authentic. The girls and I were picked to help because we teach college students about the romance writers of the early nineteenth century."

Abby Grant was an expert on Lord Byron?

The coincidence of meeting her at all, let alone here in St. Saphorin, where Auguste had made his find years ago, blew Raoul away. Excitement filled his body.

He shut off the engine so they could really talk. "You're all university professors?" He was still incredulous.

"Not tenured yet, but one day. Our goal has been to help supplement the script with new facts and a different look. There's been so much material written about Byron, but Magda has been hoping for something more. So have I."

"In what sense?"

"I'd hoped to come across a poem he was supposed to have written while he was in Switzerland. The girls dropped me off at the village library this morning so I could do a little investigating, but nothing came of it so I walked back here. Of course no one in the last one hundred and ninety years has ever pretended to find it, so maybe it doesn't exist."

This woman was not only intelligent, she had an enquiring mind that made her a very exciting person. Raoul's heart pounded like a war drum. "Did it have a title?"

"Yes. Something like *Labyrinths*, but there was another part to it. I don't know exactly."

"'Labyrinths of Lavaux'." Raoul could tell her it did exist and where to find it! Chills ran up and down his spine.

"For the last five months we've been doing research in the different parts of Europe where Byron traveled. Magda's goal is to illuminate Byron's virtues and leave the negatives alone."

"Now I understand," he murmured. "You've been following his travels here with Shelley and Mary Godwin that put the Swiss Riviera on the map."

A quiet smile curved the corners of her delectable mouth. "I can see you're well-informed. Do you want to know something funny he wrote in his journal? When he left the mountains and returned to Lac Léman he said, 'The wild part of our tour is finished...my journal must be as flat as my journey.'"

Raoul was impressed with her knowledge, but his thoughts were racing. "He could have been reading our minds right now."

"Exactly. Too much peace and tranquility needs some stirring up. Byron saw nature as a companion to humanity. Certainly natural beauty was often preferable to human evil and the problems attendant upon civilization, but Byron also recognized nature's dangerous and harsh elements.

"Have you ever read 'The Prisoner of Chillon'? It connects nature to freedom, while at the same time showing nature's potentially deadly aspects in the harsh waves that seem to threaten to flood the dungeon during a storm and—" But she suddenly stopped speaking.

"Please go on," he urged her.

"Sorry. I forgot I wasn't teaching a class. Though I'm ready to move on with the girls tomorrow, I'll never be sorry I was sent here to work. I've always had a special love for that poem."

"We're looking at the Château de Chillon right now." The lake steamer had pulled up to its dock.

She nodded. "It's a magnificent château. I've been through it half a dozen times, but after seeing the dungeon where the Swiss patriot Bonivard was imprisoned, I've been haunted by Byron's words."

"Can you quote any of it?"

Her eyes lit up. "Would you believe I memorized all 392 lines in high school for a contest?"

There was fire in her. He sat back against the side of the boat. "Did you win?"

"Would it sound like bragging if I said yes?"

She was getting to him in ways he would never have imagined. "I bet you could still recite it."

Abby shook her head. "That was too long ago."

He leaned forward. "I know I read it in my teens with my grandfather who loved Byron's works, but I would be hopeless to recall it. Come on. Give me a taste of it. We're right here where he was inspired. Enchant me."

She cocked her blond head. "Maybe some of the first part."

"I'm waiting." *Mon Dieu*—he was far too attracted to her for only having known her such a short time. Whatever was happening to him had come like a bolt out of the blue and wasn't about to go away.

Once she started to recite, the emotion she conveyed filled him with a myriad of disquieting sensations.

"My hair is grey, but not with years,
   Nor grew it white
   In a single night,
As men's have grown from sudden fears:
My limbs are bowed, though not with toil,
   But rusted with a vile repose,
For they have been a dungeon's spoil,
   And mine has been the fate of those
To whom the goodly earth and air

Are bann'd, and barr'd—forbidden fare;
But this was for my father's faith
I suffered chains and courted death;
That father perish'd at the stake
For tenets he would not forsake;
And for the same his lineal race
In darkness found a dwelling-place;
We were seven—who now are one"

The last two lines she'd recited brought back remembered pain. He could have rewritten them. 'In darkness found a dwelling place. We were three—who now are one.'

As he sat there staring at Abby, he suffered guilt for finding himself so intensely attracted to her. It seemed a betrayal to Angélique's memory. It wasn't this woman's fault—nor her desirability nor the recitation that had reached his soul, reminding him of the tragedy. He felt Abby had gone to another place too.

"Byron was a great poet," Raoul said in a voice that sounded thick to his own ears. "Thank you for bringing his words to life for a few minutes so eloquently."

She shifted in place while she looked at the château in the distance. "It hurts to know how men have been persecuted. Byron had many problems, physical and otherwise. I believe his suffering came through in that poem." Raoul felt she'd suffered too and wanted to know how.

"There's no doubt of it. No wonder you were chosen to help on the film."

She smiled. "I love what I do."

He stared hard at her. "Do you love it enough to come to France for a few days?"

A stillness washed over her. "What did you say?"

"I asked if you would like to spend some time with me at my home in Burgundy. You said your life needed a little stirring up. Your friends are welcome too."

His question seemed to have shaken her. It took her a long time before she said, "You're only saying this because you think the news about Auguste has ruined everything for us."

"Not at all. You're not the type of person to fall apart because of a change in plans. I'm quite sure your friends aren't either. That isn't the reason I've invited you."

He wanted to tell her about "Labyrinths of Lavaux" but wanted to approach her slowly. Maybe asking her to lunch would help her stay with him long enough to entertain the possibility that he was telling her the truth about his uncle's find.

She shook her head. "I don't understand."

"There's something I'd like to show you because I know you would be one person who would appreciate it. If you'll come to lunch with me, I'll give you details."

He sensed she'd try to put him off again, but after this talk on the lake, he was driven by an idea that refused to let go of him.

"If you say no after our lunch, then I'll take you back to the château and that will be the end of it."

Without waiting for a response, he started

the engine. "Louis will be happy to know this speedboat seems to be in fine working order, but I'll open up the throttle to be certain."

CHAPTER THREE

ABBY STARED AT this striking man wearing a white T-shirt and jeans. If he were featured on a billboard, the sight of him alone in whatever he wore would be worth millions for the advertisers. She found him more fantastic than any fantasy of her imagination.

"You're not a Realtor are you?"

In a few minutes, he'd pulled into the slip and turned off the engine, but the blood was still pounding in her ears. "I'm afraid that's an assumption you made."

"But you let me keep thinking it."

He slanted her one of those seductive glances he probably wasn't even aware of. "Forgive me?"

With a look like that, she could forgive him

anything and probably a lot more. That's what frightened her.

"I don't know," she finally answered him. It depends on what you do when you're not picking up strange females, at a lonely train station, no less," she went on. "In the middle of the week. In a car that looks like the one De Gaulle rode in on Bastille Day after World War II."

His quick smile took her breath.

She removed the life jacket and climbed out on her own beyond his reach. Abby felt his gaze on her and knew he was still waiting for her answer. To give in to her desire and accept his invitation would be heaven. But at what cost later on, when he no longer wanted her? After she'd sold her soul, she would never be the same again and would never be able to pick up the pieces.

"Who are you?" she blurted in panic. "*What* are you?"

"Would it help if I told you I'm a vintner?"

"From Burgundy…" She hadn't seen that coming, but she should have. Chalk it up to her being turned inside out by his male magnetism. "The clues were there. Not every Realtor knows the intimate goings-on during the pollination season at La Floraison."

"I left out one detail in my résumé. Auguste Decorvet was a distant relative of mine. The Decorvet family has many offshoots, none of them into the selling of real estate. Years ago, one of them came to Switzerland to buy a vineyard, and to get away from the dark internal fighting and struggles between family members who all wanted to be in charge."

She smiled. "I'm afraid that's true of some dynastic-minded families."

"But not yours?"

"No. My parents are quite easygoing. If I do things they don't like, they show it by being disappointed. I don't like to disappoint them."

"You're lucky to have grown up in such a household." The tone in his voice led her to believe he hadn't exaggerated his family's infighting, which probably contributed to that brooding countenance. "While we eat, you can ask me all the questions you want. But I need to know what kind of a meal will give me the answer I'm looking for from you."

"I'm afraid it's not the white fish entrées they sell along the lake."

"You really do need a change of scene."

As they walked to the car, she knew what her friends would say if she said he'd invited them to come to France for a few days. Abby had only spent a few hours with him so far.

You didn't just go off with a virtual stranger who was a vintner, even if it sounded exciting. Even if he had a legitimate familial tie with the former owner of this vineyard. Even if he had something important he wanted to show her.

But was it really so wrong if she wanted to throw caution aside and enjoy an adventure with him for as long as it lasted? To know what it would be like to lie in his arms and forget the world? Heaven help her that she was even entertaining the idea.

"I... I don't know how soon my friends will be back," her voice faltered. "If we eat in the village, they might be able to join us, depending on their timing."

"Maybe they've returned. Let's drive back to the château and check first."

When they couldn't see the red car, he drove them to a sidewalk café. They served the most divine lunch of *escalope de veau* she'd ever tasted served with peas that had to be fresh from the garden. Halfway through her *galette framboise* dessert, she put her fork down because his black eyes were studying her.

"Why are you smiling?"

"It's a pleasure to watch a woman eat a meal with enjoyment."

"I'm afraid it's not ladylike."

"According to whom?"

She didn't have to think about that one. "Other women."

"Then they're envious of your figure. If I'm being transparent, I can't help it. I'm a man."

Yes. He was a man like no other and she was growing more enamored of him by the second.

"All right. I'm waiting to hear the real reason you've invited us to come to France."

"Let me tell you a story first."

Abby. You're an idiot to sit here and listen to this any longer. This had to stop before he realized she was crazy about him.

"Raoul? Thank you for the delicious lunch. Now I think you'd better drive me back to the château." She got up from the table, but he still sat there.

"You want to leave before you're told where 'Labyrinths of Lavaux' can be found?"

With that question, she wheeled around.

"*That's* the information you wanted to tell and show me?"

"I can tell you're surprised," he came back with enviable calm. "Only Lord Byron himself. It's about the vineyards at La Floraison. When my relative Auguste Decorvet first moved into the château fifty years ago, he found it written in a notebook tucked in some *terroir* maps in the library. Perhaps Byron had stayed at the château when he was passing through years earlier."

What?

"Auguste didn't know what to think. Knowing my grandfather's English is excellent and that he has a love for Byron's works—especially those written during his Greek period—he sent the notebook to him."

Abby stood there in shock and clung to the chair back. "Your grandfather has it?"

"That's right. He thinks it's the real thing. Apparently, Byron was intrigued with the vine terracing system of the steep terrain that he called labyrinths. It's yet another example of what you were saying about the beauty, yet the harshness of nature."

Unable to stand any longer, Abby sank back down on the chair. "So he's never shown it to an expert to be authenticated?"

"No. If it was authentic, then he wanted to hold on to it and not let it be turned over to the world. I've read it. The piece only covers two notebook pages. He signed it Byron in that un-mistakable, flamboyant style.

"With Auguste gone, no one knows my grand-father has possession of it except my grand-mother, me and now you. If you'd come to France with me, he'd be honored if you would look at it and give him your expert opinion."

Abby had already made up her mind to go to France with him for a day or two. But if he was being serious about this and the poem was authentic, then this would be the most exciting event ever to happen to her.

While she was sitting there in a daze, Ginger texted that they were back. Abby let her know she'd be there in a few minutes and put the phone in her purse.

"My friends ate in Broc. I told Ginger I'd join them shortly." He wanted a yes or no answer.

"If you're telling me the truth, of course I'm tempted to meet with your grandfather and see it for myself, but—"

"But you're not sure you believe me," he broke in on her with a frankness that took her breath. He put some bills on the table and got to his feet.

She looked up at him. "After you drive us back to the farmhouse, I'll talk to my friends."

Raoul came around to help her up from the chair. She was already too sensually aware of him before she felt his hands on her shoulders. For a moment she wished he'd have pulled her into his arms. Now her legs had become traitors as he walked her out to the car.

She knew the girls had their hearts set on returning to Greece and Italy. They wouldn't want to go to France and would laugh at her for being so gullible. She knew they'd question her sanity if she took Raoul up on his invitation.

Her thoughts were more than prophetic when a half hour later, after she'd introduced them to Raoul in the courtyard, they went upstairs to her bedroom. She told them everything, including the fact that he was a widower who'd lost his child too.

Zoe eyed her with compassion. "I understand the attraction. He's gorgeous and has a male virulence no woman could be immune to. But maybe he's a little too clever. Once you told him about the supposed missing work of Lord Byron and mentioned the name *Labyrinths*, it wouldn't have been that difficult for him to fill in the word *Lavaux*, right?"

"I was thinking the same thing," Ginger murmured. "What I don't understand is why he feels he has to bribe you. A man as attractive as he is could get his way with a woman anytime without using subterfuge to entice her. He must want you to go with him very badly."

Not as badly as I want to go.

"That's what I'm thinking," Zoe concluded. "I don't think I could do it, but I guess it all depends on how much he means to you already."

Abby averted her eyes. "You guys would be shocked if you knew the intensity of my feelings."

"If they're that strong, then all I can say is, don't let him hurt you like Nigel did."

Heat filled Abby's cheeks. "That's my dilemma, Ginger. I don't want to get involved with him, yet I'm so drawn to him, I can hardly bear the thought of never seeing him again."

"Then it sounds like you've made up your mind to go with him."

"I don't know. I believe he's telling the truth, and he has invited you guys to come too. We could all take a look at it."

"If it exists," Ginger interjected. "But let's face it. You want to be with him, whether he has something to show you or not, right?"

"Yes," she whispered, "but I need more time to think about it. Why don't you two take off for Italy so I don't hold you up. I'm going to have another talk with Raoul this afternoon. If I decide it's not worth the risk, I'll fly from Geneva to Venice and meet you there tomorrow. How does that sound?"

Zoe smiled. "Whatever you decide, we're behind you."

"Just be careful," Ginger cautioned before they all hugged.

Since they'd already packed the night before,

there was nothing to do but walk them out to the rental car. "We'll phone each other every day."

"Absolument," Abby assured them with one of the French words she loved and waved them off. Then she walked back in the farmhouse to phone Raoul from her bedroom phone. Her heart beat so hard in her throat she could hardly ask Gabrielle to put her through to him.

"Abby—" came his deep voice. "I was wondering if I'd hear back from you. What's the verdict?"

Maybe she'd regret this, but she couldn't stop herself. She longed to be with him and nothing else mattered. "The girls have already left for Italy."

"Which means they don't believe what I told you."

She gripped the phone tighter. "They want me to make up my own mind."

"And have you?"

"Yes. The likening of the vineyards to labyrinths sounded…Byronic. Not every charlatan is that clever."

There was silence on the other end for a few seconds. "How soon can you be ready to travel and finding out if that label fits me?"

"I'm ready now. If I come with you, it will only be for an overnight. Once I've seen the notebook, I'll be leaving for Italy."

"I admire you for being more open-minded than your friends."

Or so much more foolish.

"I'll pick you up outside in five minutes."

"In what?"

"It won't be the Renault."

"I'm sure Gabrielle and Louis will be relieved. So will I. I wasn't sure it was going to make it back from the village."

Abby hung up on his chuckle and hurried to call Gabrielle to thank her for everything. Once that was done, she reached for her suitcase and walked down the stairs, wondering what on earth had come over her. How could she be this excited when she might be welcoming a heartache that could mean her ruination? But somehow it didn't matter.

When she opened the doors, Abby didn't know what she expected. But it wasn't the metallic blue Maserati GranTurismo convertible sitting in the courtyard with the top down.

A car like that cost close to two hundred thousand dollars. Her gaze met Raoul's. "Where did this come from?"

"I parked it around the other side of the château." He reached for her suitcase and put it in the backseat. "I like the sun and the wind, but I'll raise the top if you prefer."

"No, please—I love a convertible!"

A heart-stopping white smile broke out on his tanned face. "A woman who doesn't mind getting her hair mussed."

"Give it time."

Little did she know when she'd had her hair cut that she'd be thankful for the short style while he drove her to France. She felt his eyes on her legs as he helped her into the passenger side. Abby was glad she was wearing jeans.

Every look, every slight touch made her come alive. When he got behind the wheel, he angled a piercing glance at her. "We'll be home in three hours. Fasten your seat belt."

Abby's misgivings about getting in over her head intensified as they wound around to the E23. It was too late to back out now. For a little while neither of them talked as they headed in a northwestern direction toward France. He drove with the expertise of a race car driver.

They stopped at the border for a cola and some madeleines. She could have brushed her hair, but didn't see the point since they'd be off again in a few minutes.

He ate a couple of the cookies. "These are some of my favorites."

"I like them too. Would you tell me where we're going exactly in Burgundy?"

"To my home outside the village of Vosne-Romanée. It's near the city of Dijon. The Regnac Capet Decorvet Domaine was founded in 1475 by my family twenty generations ago."

"How wonderful to have a family history that dates back so far." This man had an amazing heritage. But he also had a heartache no one could forget or totally recover from.

"When my great-grandfather died, my grandfather became the head of the corporation. He's still alive, but because of their old age and maladies, he and my grandmother keep to their own suite in the château with nurses and a health care giver taking care of them.

"My father, Étienne, the eldest child, was made the head, but unfortunately he's been stricken with an aggressive form of arthritis and is in a wheelchair. My mother, Hélène-Claire, and a health care giver look after him. Because of his condition, he made me the head of the corporation a year ago.

"But my uncles Pierre and Lucien, and my aunts Mireille and Abeline, along with their spouses and children, have been upset about my ascension and have a great deal to say about every move I make."

"Why is that?"

"As I told you earlier, everyone in the family wants to be in charge."

"But that doesn't make sense."

"You're right, so don't even try."

There had to be more to it than that. "It sounds like the Decorvet dynasty has been prolific," she observed. "That *is* a lot of family. Do they all live close by?"

"For those not living in the château, they're too close."

"Which king was it who complained to his minister that he had no friends, and the minister said, 'Of course not. You're the king!'?"

"Where did you acquire such wisdom?" he murmured, but she heard him.

"Do you have siblings?"

"Two. My sister, Josette, is married to Paul. They have a three-year-old boy Maurice, and are expecting their second child. My brother, Jean-Marc, is still single and works in the exporting office for our corporation with Uncle Pierre. Everyone is involved in some way in the family business, thus the friction."

Abby remembered his telling her about the relative that left for Switzerland because of the dark side of his family's relationships. The one who'd found the supposed notebook with Byron's writing. Friction was no doubt the polite description of what went on within the Decorvet inner circle.

"As I see it, your family can't help but have difficult moments. It's natural because they work in the same business." She shook her head. "That would never work for my family.

"Tell me about yours."

"I have aunts and uncles on both sides," Abby informed him, "but they don't work with my dad. He runs an insurance agency and my mom works for a hospital in medical records. My brother, Steve, just finished law school and my older sister, Nadine, is pregnant with her third child.

"I have four cousins and everyone is a free thinker. Thank goodness there aren't any secrets to be kept under lock and key, like a secret recipe for the wine *you* produce. No one would be able to keep quiet." Low laughter rumbled out of Raoul.

"What kind of wine do you make?"

"The only grape we grow is the pinot noir. Nothing but *grand cru*."

"What does that mean?"

"That it's superior quality. The earth here has an exceptional purity."

"Why?"

"Because it's made up of red-brown clay and large bits of limestone. The soil drains so well that the flavors are kept concentrated and powerful. It's known that this area's soil takes our crop to a new extreme of depth and concentration, producing a one-of-a-kind wine."

Abby heard pride in his voice. "How much does your wine cost?"

"I'm afraid the bottles are priced at extravagant levels. Depending on weather conditions, we sell three hundred thousand bottles yearly from seven different *terroirs*."

She finished her drink. "Is that a lot?"

"Not really."

His answer proved she knew nothing about his work, but she was fascinated by everything she'd learned so far. "I've only been told a little about the *chalessas* grape variety that grows around Lac Léman."

One dark brow lifted. "Then you know more than most tourists. And I've told you more than most people will ever know about my family, so we don't have to talk about it again."

She knew he meant it. Then his half smile appeared and her heart jumped.

They drove back to the motorway. Now that they were on French soil, the signs and architecture were different. When they reached Dijon, she exclaimed over the fabulous *toits bourguignons*. Raoul explained that their polychrome roofs were made of tiles glazed in green, yellow, black and terracotta. They'd been arranged in geometric patterns. Abby took pictures with her phone.

Before long Raoul gave her a tour as they followed the sign for Vosne-Romanée, teaching her about the area and its wonders with every kilometer. They drove past many lush *terroirs* of vineyards growing on the limestone slopes of the Côte d'Or escarpment.

"It's evident Gauguin never traveled here, Raoul. He would have had a field day painting the landscape of Vosne-Romanée—the different *terroirs*, hedges, trees and gardens all arranged like a great patchwork in his unmistakable style. I have to tell you I'm entranced."

"So am I by every word that comes out of your mouth."

Like an underwater geyser, his comment sent steaming heat through her body. Abby could feel his magic getting to her. It frightened her that she was so susceptible to him. Too much longer in his company and she'd never want to leave. He'd had such a cataclysmic effect on her, how would she be able to bear it if it turned out his feelings for her blew hot, then cold because she could never take the place of his beloved wife?

Eventually they came to a tall ornate grillwork gate. At the top it said, Regnac-Capet Decorvet

Domaine. But her attention was caught by the coat of arms beneath the words.

Her gaze flew to his. "Was this a royal property at one time?"

He took his time before he said, "My ancestor was a duke from the House of Burgundy."

Bits and pieces of unassociated information flew at her while she started piecing them together. Talk about a patchwork. But this one added up to a canvas so extraordinary, she started trembling and couldn't speak for a minute. Yesterday when he'd appeared like a Gallic prince out of one of her dreams, she'd known something in her world had changed.

"You're a duke, aren't you?"

CHAPTER FOUR

"THE OBSOLETE TITLE belongs to my grandfather."

"But when he and your father die, you'll inherit it."

"It won't mean a thing."

"Except in your family's mind, I'd wager."

Good heavens. Raoul wasn't just the head of a famous Burgundian family. He was a titled aristocrat, too removed from ordinary life for her to imagine being any part of it. And two years ago he'd lost his wife and child. It was only natural that he had a man's appetites and needs and had found himself attracted to Abby on his trip. It didn't mean anything.

But he wasn't your typical male. A brief relationship was all that could come of their being together. She'd have tonight with him, but tomorrow she would leave and fly to Italy while she still had the strength to tear herself away.

He pressed a remote on his keys and the doors swung open. They passed through and continued along a drive lined with trees and velvety green lawns. But when he turned to the right, she gasped, not prepared for what awaited her.

Set among the foliage lay an enormous ochre-toned château. The sides with their turrets book-ended a middle section where there was one of those geometric patterns of tiles on the roofs covering the three stories of mullioned glass windows.

This was the ancestral home of the Frenchman who'd climbed out of the old Renault at the train station yesterday? It was no longer a mystery why he hadn't come for one pitiful stranded tourist in his Maserati. Unpeeling his many layers needed to happen in increments.

"I'll give you the grand tour of the whole estate by car first, then I'll feed you." He kept on driving. In the distance she saw a helicopter on a landing pad. The ancient and the modern, side by side.

They continued along a private road behind the château where there was a miniature structure built along the same lines as the château with a pond in front.

Beyond it were many outbuildings and vineyards in the distance where the estate employees processed and stored the wine. There had to be hundreds of workers to keep it all going. "This is like a town within a town that has grown from the Middle Ages. My parents' home in San José was built twenty-five years ago. We thought *it* was old."

"America is a young country."

"Have you been there?"

"Several times."

Of course he had.

He followed the road around, making a loop. "You see those vines to the south? They're young, under twenty-five years old. We don't include them in our *premier cru* bottling."

"Why not?"

"Because it takes the vines that long to express the greatness of the *terroir* where they are planted. My grandfather taught me that the young vines remain young vines, however fine the grapes they produce. To quote him, 'They're like you gifted teenagers.'"

"Your grandfather sounds kind." The warmth in his voice revealed his affection for him.

"I plan on your meeting him and my grandmother. Your sense of humor and your knowledge of Lord Byron will appeal to him."

"Why does he love Byron's writing so much?"

"My grandfather had a dog he named Vercingetorix in honor of the most notable Gallic warrior who fought against Caesar. After his dog died, he happened to come across Lord Byron's, 'Epitaph to a Dog,' and he wept. That started his love for the poet. He read everything."

Abby nodded. "Like 'The Prisoner of Chillon,' that's another piece that touches your heart. Byron had been devoted to his dog, not caring it had rabies. He nursed it without worrying about infection."

"My grandfather used to add his own words, 'All the virtues of man without his vices.'"

At this point she was positive she would wake up at any moment to discover Raoul was not only bigger than life, he was a figment of her imagination. He drove them back toward the château, but he stopped in front of what he called the *petit château* by the pond.

"I'm sure you need to freshen up. Let's go inside and I'll show you to your apartment while you're here. This is used when we have important guests who must stay overnight. The *grand château* is a relic, too museum-like and formal to enjoy. One day soon I'll take you on a tour of it, but I guarantee you'll much prefer staying here in privacy and modernized comfort."

There wouldn't be another day after tomorrow with him. She was leaving as soon as he let her take a look at the notebook, *if* there was such a thing. To stay any longer would be a mistake she would never recover from. Her mind could tell her she'd come with him to see if this work really was Byron's. But her heart had a mind of its own where the man himself was concerned.

The apartment turned out to be a home within a home, lavish enough for a queen with every accoutrement imaginable, including a kitchen with anything she'd want to eat or drink. Raoul carried in her suitcase and set it down on the exquisite parquet flooring. They exchanged cell phone numbers.

"I'll be back for you in an hour and we'll go out for dinner." He disappeared behind the French doors too fast for her to say goodbye.

The conversation with Ginger rang in her ears. *What I don't understand is why he feels he has to bribe you. A man as attractive as he is could get his way with a woman anytime without using subterfuge to entice her. He must want you to go with him very badly.*

What was the truth? Did he want to be with Abby beyond logic or reason? That's the way she felt about him, but she couldn't honestly answer her own question. She didn't *want* to answer it because if the truth didn't match the

man she thought he was, she knew it would dev-
astate her to the point she'd never get over it.

After he left, she unpacked her suitcase. The
task only took a few minutes. She showered and
put on a *café-au-lait*-colored sundress with a
short-sleeved white jacket. Once she'd brushed
her hair and put on lipstick, she went back outside full of nervous energy while she waited for
Raoul's call and drank in her lush green surroundings.

With rose bushes in bloom and lily pads dec-
orating the picturesque pond, she felt like she'd
walked into a Monet painting. Her mind kept
going over the things he'd told her about his
family. He had responsibilities she couldn't
imagine. As she leaned over to smell one of
the brilliant pink roses, she saw a figure.

Coming from the direction of the *grand
château* she watched a man stride toward her
dressed in a pullover and trousers. He had a
certain look that reminded her of Raoul. They
seemed close in age, but he wasn't quite as tall.

"Eh, bien." His dark brown eyes played over

her with what she felt was an interest a little too familiar. *"Puis-je vous aider?"*

"Pardon me?" She pretended not to understand him. She understood that much French, but she didn't want to get into a conversation with Raoul's brother.

"Ah. *Americaine.* I thought my eyes were deceiving me when I stepped out of the château and saw a beautiful woman standing there. Where did *you* come from?" His French accent wasn't as pronounced as Raoul's. Because this must be Raoul's brother, she needed to be careful what she said.

"I'm a tourist from California."

He continued to appraise her with an undoubtedly practiced smile that would work on most women. Jean-Marc had his own brand of charm. "I spent time there when I was in the States. What part?"

"San José."

"I'm afraid I only made it to the Napa Valley. May I know your name, *mademoiselle*?"

"Abby Grant."

He put his hands on his hips. "You must be here with a buyer. I wasn't aware we were expecting one this late in the day. If you'll allow me, I'd be happy to show you around while you're being kept waiting."

The man didn't waste time. He was a huge flirt. "That's very nice of you, but I don't even know your name."

A shocked laugh burst out of him. "Jean-Marc Decorvet."

"Ah." She smiled. "When Raoul arrives in a minute, I'll tell him I met his brother."

In an instant, the mention of his sibling wiped the smile from his good-looking face. Judging by that unhappy reaction, Raoul hadn't exaggerated about the dynamics in his family. "How do you know him?" It might have been a normal question, except that he sounded upset. Maybe that wasn't the word, exactly. She didn't understand.

"We met while I was on vacation."

He acted stunned. "Where?"

It wasn't his business, but she didn't want to

offend Raoul's brother. "Switzerland." As politely as possible she said, "It's very nice to meet you. Maybe we'll see each other again."

On that note Abby continued to walk toward the vineyards in the distance. She felt his eyes on her back, but never turned around.

Please call me soon, Raoul.

After Raoul had left Abby, he'd driven by the main *domaine* office on the estate to check in with Félix. His dependable forty-year-old secretary hadn't left for home yet. He looked pleased to see Raoul. "I'm glad you're back."

"I'm sure your wife is too."

He smiled. "You were gone five days too long. When you're away, it gets like a madhouse around here."

"That's why I leave everything in your capable hands. How did it go with Jules?"

"He assured me he took care of the spraying."

"Bon."

"Solange de la Croix Godard has come by every day expecting to see you back. She hopes you haven't forgotten the Regional Wine Association Dinner tomorrow night."

"No."

But Raoul had never made plans to take her. She could hope, but that was a fiction she and her parents had dreamed up. Since his trip to St. Saphorin, he had other plans.

Meeting Abby had changed his world. Yesterday he'd experienced a *coup de foudre*. Raoul had never given any credence to two people falling in love at first sight, but there was no other explanation for what had happened to them. It surpassed any reservations he might have had thanks to his guilt about Angélique.

She'd felt it too, otherwise she wouldn't have come with him even though she'd tried to fight it. He needed and wanted her in his life no matter what.

"Anything else, Félix?"

His secretary started to say something, then changed his mind. Raoul didn't need to know the reason why. "What did my brother do now?"

"It's what your uncle Pierre mentioned to me. I don't know how important it is."

"If that were true, you wouldn't have that frustrated look on your face."

"I understand Jean-Marc tried to handle a possible new client from Denmark while you were gone, but he quoted a lower price to seal the deal without checking with Pierre until it was too late."

That sounded like Jean-Marc. His unhappy twenty-nine-year-old brother was only a year younger than Raoul, and had always resented the fact that Raoul would have first claim to the title once their grandfather and father passed away. Things had gotten worse since their father had chosen Raoul to take over the company a year ago—another nail in the coffin. Jean-Marc had always made everything into a competition—work, sports, women. The situation wasn't going to improve anytime soon.

Raoul needed to talk to their autocratic father. If Jean-Marc were to be given total control over some aspect of the business, it might help him feel more important.

"Thanks for telling me. I'll speak with Pierre. Anything else?"

"Yes. The funeral of André Laroche. I was informed it's set for tomorrow at twelve at the church."

One of their best employees had suffered a fatal heart attack. "I'll be attending as no doubt will some of the members of the family."

"Shall I arrange to get flowers sent?"

"I've already taken care of it, Félix."

He nodded. "Was your trip to Switzerland successful?"

"Very." Raoul was elated that Abby had come to Burgundy with him and was staying in the *petit château* a short distance away. Tomorrow he'd show her the piece written by Byron and get that out of the way. Then they'd take advantage of the time to love each other. He was living for that.

"Go on home to your wife and take the day off tomorrow. You deserve it."

Félix blinked, which wasn't surprising. Raoul had never been in love until now. The feelings he was experiencing now defied description and his secretary sensed it.

Raoul left the *domaine* headquarters for home. Since the deaths of his wife and child, he'd moved out of the *grand château* to a small, vacant cottage on the property he'd had renovated to suit him. He liked the distance it gave him from the family. It had allowed him to grieve in private for losing his daughter and for not loving his wife the way he should have.

From the day he'd married her, his emotions had been raw with regret for their marriage, which should never have taken place. It had torn him apart. Yet the guilt he'd always felt because he'd never wanted Angélique, hadn't stopped him from bringing Abby here now. It seemed a betrayal, but he couldn't suppress his desire to be with her as he hurried to the cottage to shower and change for dinner.

Of course word had gotten out that he was back. While he was dressing in a silky sport shirt and trousers, he had four phone calls. One from his parents, one from his sister, plus two others from his Aunt Abeline and her son, Gilles. He knew exactly what the latter two wanted. This was one time he decided to have it out with his cousin.

"Bonsoir, Gilles."

"Sorry to bother you when you just got back, but Maman wants to know what's happened to the Floraison property."

Abeline wasn't the only one interested. Gilles, divorced and low on funds, wanted it for himself. Once he got it, he'd sell it and gamble away the money. "I'm afraid it's been sold."

"What? When she hears that, she won't stand for it."

Gilles was as transparent as glass. "She'll have to."

"Then she'll get an attorney and fight you."

"It won't matter. The attorney of record followed Auguste's will to the letter. No member of the Decorvet family can be the new buyer. I only went to Switzerland to arrange for a few of Auguste's things to be shipped back to the estate. Tell her that when you talk to her. Since I'm in a hurry, it will save my having to call her back. *Au revoir, Gilles.*"

The calls to his parents and Josette could wait. Since he'd become a widower, the one thing on their minds was to force him into a marriage with Solange. With the help of her father, they all assumed it was a *fait accompli* in the making. How little they knew what went on inside Raoul…

Without hesitation, he rang Abby who answered on the second ring. "Raoul?"

"Sorry I've been longer than an hour."

"It's all right. I realize you've come home to business."

"I'm through dealing with the emergencies. If you're ready, I'll pick you up in front of your accommodations."

"Not there—I took a walk past some of the vineyards beyond the pond while I was waiting. I'm starting back now and will watch for you on the main drive."

"I'll find you. What kind of dinner are you in the mood for?"

"Surprise me with the type of local food you enjoy."

He'd never met a woman with a nature like hers. Abby was charming, educated, bright, funny and so damn attractive. But she was planning to fly to Italy after she'd seen the notebook.

The thought of her going anywhere was anathema to him. But he needed to be careful. He knew she didn't trust him completely yet. The sooner she saw what she'd come to see, the sooner he could carry out his plans for them to explore what could be between them.

After hanging up, he left the cottage and walked around the back to get in his ten-year-old black Jaguar. He preferred to take the convertible on trips, but used his older car around the village for business.

When he caught up to her, Abby had walked quite a distance on her long, slender legs. Though the sky had clouded over, she stood out from her surroundings. Raoul's gaze took in the sheen of her silky blond hair, which the breeze had disheveled. His eyes couldn't help but follow her womanly shape clothed in a sundress that looked made for her.

He slowed down when he reached her. At first she stared at the car without recognition. "Have you changed your mind about dinner?"

Then her eyes, green and alive, met his. In that moment he knew she was excited to see him.

"Oh—it's *you*!" She hurried around and got in the car, bringing the scent of her strawberry shampoo fragrance with her. "I didn't know you had another car. I love the British pronunciation of this one. Jag-u-*ar*. You must think I'm crazy. I don't know why I like the sounds of certain words. It's a quirk of mine."

Raoul didn't think she was crazy. "I like your quirks." He turned the car around and they drove out of the estate beyond the gate to the road that would take them into the village. It was then he heard a sigh from her that sounded troubled. "What's wrong?"

"Not wrong, but there's something I should tell you."

He knew it. The last twenty-four hours had been too good to be true. "I presume you had a phone call from your friends. They think I've preyed on you and now you believe it."

"That's not it," she muttered.

He pulled over to the side of the road. "Can you look me in the eye and tell me you never once wondered if I'd been lying to you?"

She moistened her lips nervously. "No. I believed you."

"Then let's start again. Something's bothering you. Have you decided you don't want to stay here after all?"

Her head turned in his direction. "Anyone who didn't want to stay here would have to be comatose."

"But?"

"While I was walking by the pond, I met your brother."

A grimace marred his features. That was all he had to hear to understand.

"He said he thought I'd come to the estate with a buyer and offered to show me around while I waited. I thanked him, but told him I was waiting for you. His shocked reaction surprised me."

Abby's instincts were right on. His brother wouldn't have believed Raoul had invited a woman to come to the estate for personal reasons. He knew Raoul had been in mourning since the funeral.

Jean-Marc would be inordinately curious over what was going on. It was only natural that his brother would have taken one look at Abby and decided to make her his next conquest.

"What did you tell him?"

"I gave him my name and told him I was a tourist from California. He wanted to know how we met. I told him it was in Switzerland, but of course I didn't say anything else."

"I hope he didn't make you uncomfortable."

"No." She was searching for the right words. "He just seemed…caught off guard and curious."

"That's his nature." But the knowledge that

Raoul had invited Abby here was one bomb-shell his brother wouldn't have seen coming in a million years. Like the rest of the family, Jean-Marc always wanted to know Raoul's personal business and tried to anticipate his next move. His grandparents were the exception.

"Is he older or younger than you?"

Raoul wanted to get off the subject. "He's twenty-nine, younger than me by a year."

"Almost like twins."

"Not quite." Jean-Marc and Gilles were the ones who resembled each other in certain be-haviors. "Let's just say we have a difficult his-tory and let it go at that." He gripped the wheel tighter and drove back on to the road.

"Where are you taking us?"

Raoul gave her another sideward glance. "Any place to get away from the claustrophobic world I live in."

"I guess you can get claustrophobic in a châ-teau the size of yours, or a one room dwelling, depending on the company."

Abby was incredibly easy to talk to.

The Petite Auberge Blanche served a good meal he thought she'd like. He pulled into the parking and escorted her inside the busy establishment, cupping her elbow. The owner knew him from boyhood.

His eyes rounded in surprise because Raoul hadn't brought in a woman since long before his wife's death. The older man, all smiles, showed them to a table outside on the terrace where a group was playing the kind of soft rock music that catered to tourists. Some were dancing. He sent a waiter over to take their orders and serve them the house wine.

Since touching her, Raoul needed more physical contact. "Would you like to dance?"

"I'm not very good at it."

He was getting used to her refusing him, but it wasn't going to work. "At least in this case you don't need a life preserver. Just hold on to me."

CHAPTER FIVE

SOMEHOW RAOUL GOT his way with Abby because she'd fallen headlong in love with him. There was no way to avoid what was right in front of her. When she felt his arms go around her, all coherent thought ceased.

Though she needed to fight her attraction to him, when he pulled her against him, she enjoyed it too much. She stood five-seven in her low wedges and felt made for him as he moved her around the floor with his face resting in her hair.

No man could equal Raoul in looks or demeanor. Though his expensive charcoal silk shirt and black trousers distinguished him from the other males in the restaurant, it was the very essence of him that caused every female to follow him with their eyes.

His solid, powerful legs brushed against hers, sending curls of desire through her body. That's when the alarm bells went off. She didn't dare let this go on for fear everyone in the room could see they needed more privacy.

"The waiter has brought out our food, Raoul," she whispered. "We'd better go back to the table before it gets cold."

His hands tightened on her upper arms before he relinquished his hold on her, as if he didn't want to let her go. She hadn't wanted this to stop either.

He walked her back to the table laden with their meal: escargot, baked duck in honey, skewered pork tenderloin marinated in red pesto with sweet chorizo, creamy risotto and apple tart for dessert.

"Are you trying to fatten me up?" she teased later to keep things on a lighter note. The band had taken a break that stopped any dancing for a little while.

His gaze narrowed on her features. "If it keeps you happy."

She paused before taking another sip of wine. "You think I'm not?"

"I know you're waiting to see that notebook. We'll visit my grandparents tomorrow. In the meantime, I'd like to show you a part of the château that might interest you."

That probably meant they'd be together alone. Abby put the goblet down with a trembling hand. "I'd like that."

His touch was electric as he walked her back to the car.

Raoul didn't speak while they drove to the estate and passed through the gate. Instead of parking in front of the *petit château*, he took another route that circled around the *grand château*. They wound up at a back entrance.

"I've brought you to my office, one of two places on the estate where I have completely privacy. The other is the cottage where I live." He helped her out of the car.

"You don't stay in the château?"

"Not anymore. After the funeral, I needed to live strictly alone."

"I can understand that," she whispered. He and his wife must have had a great love. At times the memories had to torture him.

He opened the door and let them inside. "This room was once known as *le Salon de Dionysos*, the Greek god of wine. For a hundred years it was used during the yearly *vendange*, what you would call the grape harvest. But last year I claimed it for my *Saint des Saints*."

"What does that mean?"

"I believe you refer to it as your inner sanctum."

Abby liked the sound of it in French. After he turned on a few lights, she started to walk around the huge vaulted room. She was speechless. It had been modernized to create a state-of-the-art office with comfortable furniture.

But everywhere she looked on the walls and ceilings were colorful scenes of the famous god riding on the back of a panther or walking through a pine forest with an ivy wreath on his curly head. In another section Dionysus was being pulled in a chariot by a pair of beasts.

She rolled her eyes at him. "This room is so spectacular I don't see how you get any work done. When you were a little boy, you must have been in heaven running around in here. I don't have to see the rest of the château to know it has to be one of Burgundy's treasures."

He'd been checking information on his computer. "A costly one. Last year France's grape harvest was among the smallest in thirty years, down ten percent from the year before."

She frowned. "That has to be troubling news to every vintner."

"Especially for those who haven't modernized. For the last ten years I've been navigating through the high-tech investments necessary to keep this place going. When I lift my eyes, the decor in here keeps me grounded to my roots and reminds me of what is important."

"Taking care of your family means you carry a heavy weight on your shoulders." Plus the terrible personal tragedy that had to have been so devastating for him.

"I'm not complaining. I simply want us to understand each other better."

So did Abby who didn't know nearly enough about him. She walked over to one of the upholstered chairs near the massive fireplace and sat down.

Raoul's black eyes gleamed in the soft light as he moved toward her and perched on the end of the couch next to her. "I realize you don't trust me yet."

"We hardly know each other."

"I'm afraid I've expected too much from you."

For him to admit to any vulnerability came as a complete surprise. "Now I'm going to ask *you* what's wrong."

He made a strange sound in his throat. "I shouldn't have brought you to the estate."

Her breath caught. "Because there's no notebook after all?"

In the next instant Raoul's hand shot out to cover hers. "You know there is," his voice grated. "And you *know* that's not what I meant!"

A tiny nerve throbbed at the corner of his compelling mouth.

"I'm sorry I said that."

"You had every right. Would it shock you if I told you I wanted to bring you back with me from the moment I saw you sitting on the bench at the train station? But life on the estate is like living in a fish bowl. I would spare you that if I could."

"Well, that can be easily remedied," she said to hide the sudden stab of pain she knew he hadn't inflicted on purpose. "I'll stay at a hotel in the village tonight and leave for Venice tomorrow as planned."

"Without seeing the poem you came to look at?"

"Raoul—you're confusing me. Do I seem that emotionally fragile to you?"

He removed his hand and shook his dark, handsome head. "Of course not. But there's an untouched purity about you I can't put into words."

"Pure—that's the way you see me?"

"You're the most real woman I've ever met. No pretense or affectation. I don't want that unique quality of yours to be blighted because of your relationship with me."

"Spoken like a vintner," she said to lighten his mood, but it didn't work. "We don't have a relationship, Raoul."

"But we could have one," he fired back. "I've told you about Angélique and the baby, but you haven't shared a word about yourself. Is that because there's someone else waiting for you when you return to the States? A man who wouldn't like it to know you were here with me?"

She lifted her eyes. "No. No one."

He raked a hand through his black hair. "Even if there isn't, there have to have been many men who wanted a relationship with you."

"Many?" She shook her head. "I've known two men whom I thought I could marry."

"Why didn't either of them work out?"

"When I was twenty and an undergraduate, I met a guy called Jim while on vacation in Carmel. He was a fun and easy-going cowboy from

Nevada who lived on a cattle ranch. I eventually met his family and spent some time with him there. But hard as I tried, I couldn't see myself adapting to the life he adored. It was obvious I didn't love him enough."

Raoul cocked his dark head. "You were young."

"True. Four years later I met Nigel, a visiting professor from Cambridge, England. We worked together for two semesters. I fell in love with his accent first."

Raoul smiled. "One of your quirks."

"Yes, then I fell for him. He was brilliant and fascinating and wanted to marry me. Right before Christmas break we were planning a spring wedding. While he was teaching a class, a woman came in to his office. She claimed to be his wife and showed me pictures of the two of them with their children.

"Needless to say, I told him I never wanted to see him again. You don't need to know how ugly it was. But after that experience, I don't want to be hurt again like that. Not ever."

"I'm sorry you've been through that kind of pain," he murmured in a voice filled with a compassion she felt through to her insides. "Is that how you ended up in Switzerland?"

She looked up and searched Raoul's eyes. "When I went to the head of the department and asked for a leave of absence, he told me I could do some research for Magda until the summer, and that brought me to Switzerland."

"*Dieu merci* it did. But after what you've been through, I'm surprised you agreed to drive here with me."

"Frankly, so am I, even with the prize you dangled in front of me."

"That prize does exist, but whether it's authentic will be for you to decide."

Abby eyed him seriously. "Assuming you've told me the truth about your life so far, what was it about your wife that made you want to marry her? Why did it work for you?"

He took time answering. "Angélique de Dampierre was attractive and born into an aristocratic Burgundian wine family. Our family had known hers all our lives, but I didn't begin spending time with her until three years ago. That was at the time when my father's arthritis was advancing.

"One evening after a party where the Dampierre family was in attendance, he took me aside. In private he told me he was stepping down as the head of the estate and would be making me the head. I knew he'd been cultivating me for that position from the cradle. What I didn't know was that he expected me to marry Angélique."

Abby sat there in stunned disbelief. "Are you saying you entered into an arranged marriage?"

Raoul nodded. "He and René Dampierre had talked it over years earlier. The union of our two families would ensure stability and bring financial security for years to come. But my father said I had to be married first and Angélique, with her aristocratic background, would make the perfect vintner's wife."

"That sounds so feudal."

"If you knew my father, nothing would surprise you. Once in a while the ruthless side comes out in him, making him a formidable opponent. I had no plan to marry anyone at the time and told him he should make Jean-Marc the heir. We had some violent quarrels and I threatened to leave the estate and move to Paris.

"In fact I was in the process of packing my bags when my mother got hold of me and posed an argument that forced me to listen. The doctor had told her my father didn't have more than a year to live. She couldn't abide anyone else in our difficult family taking over once he was gone. She said it had to be me in charge or the Decorvet estate would fall into ruin.

"My mother is a shrewd woman with a will of iron. She comes from an old aristocratic wine family too. She understands what it takes to keep the family on top. I knew deep down as I listened to her that she was speaking the truth. Once my father passed away, there would be chaos. My grandfather couldn't possibly run things, and he'd die watching his fifty years of unceasing work as the patriarch fall apart."

"So you married Angélique," Abby whispered.

There was a silence before he said, "It didn't go well."

"Did she know how you felt?"

"I'm sure she did."

"But she married you anyway because she wanted to be your wife."

At least he didn't try to say that she was following orders too. No doubt Angélique had been in love with him for years.

"My father got what he wanted, and then miraculously didn't die. He's still alive trying to run things even though he put me in charge. I wouldn't put it past him to have bribed the doctor to lie about his condition in order to get his way."

"I can't comprehend a parent doing that."

"What saved any of this for me was the birth of our little girl Nicolette. She was two and half months at the time of the crash."

A groan came out of Abby. She wished she hadn't asked him about his marriage. She knew he would always be in pain over that. "I'm so sorry for your loss." Raoul hadn't been married to Angélique very long. Even if it hadn't been the ideal marriage or anything close, how could one get over losing both of them in such a horrid way?

What kind of a dream world had Abby been living in to drive here with this fabulous, enigmatic, important man in order to see something possibly written by Lord Byron? What was she hoping for now? That Raoul would fall desperately in love with her? That she'd live happily ever after with a man this tormented by family problems and tragedy?

Abby should never have mentioned his wife. She looked around the room that shouted as nothing else could how foreign his world and aristocratic background was to hers. She could never be his *raison d'être*. Abby needed to leave for Italy tomorrow, no matter what.

Unable to sit there any longer, she stood up. "Thank you for dinner and the opportunity to see the Salon de Dionysos. I feel very privileged that you would allow me a glimpse inside your

Saint des Saints." She'd tried to pronounce it correctly. "But it's getting late and I'm positive you're tired after our long drive today. I'd better go back to my room."

Lines darkened his striking features. "Now that I've been honest with you, why do I get the feeling you're running away from me already?"

He could see through her with those piercing black eyes. She started to tremble. "Because I'm questioning my own judgment. Since we arrived at the estate, nothing feels right."

"That's because what we felt for each other when we first met was like a clap of thunder out of a blue sky. I was reminded of a line in 'The Young Fools' by Verlaine."

"What line was that?" She'd enjoyed much of the French poet's translated work.

"Suddenly a white nape flashed beneath the branches, and this sight was a delicate feast for a young fool's heart."

"Raoul—" Where had he pulled that from? He never ceased to amaze her.

"The reverberations have been growing stronger with every passing minute, so don't deny it." He got up from the couch and reached for her with his strong hands. Their mouths were only centimeters apart.

"I don't deny it, but I'm not looking for any kind of complication. I never want to go through the pain of betrayal again."

She heard his sharp intake of breath. "I'm positive my father lied to me to get his own way. You think I don't understand betrayal?"

Abby shook her head, not immune to the tortured tone in his voice. "I don't know what to think," she cried.

"Then don't," he said before covering her mouth with a kiss so hungry and full of desire that she moaned. Finding herself immersed in sensations her body had never known before, she slid her hands up the silk covering his chest and wrapped her arms around his neck.

As Abby began kissing him back, she was overwhelmed by her need for him and what he was doing to her. She couldn't get close enough to him. The thought of his stopping was agony.

He rubbed her back and hips, molding her to him. "*Mon Dieu*, you have no idea what you do to me," he whispered against her lips. "To think I almost put off going to Switzerland until the end of the month."

"I shouldn't have come with you. My friends warned me, but I couldn't help myself. Verlaine was right about young fools."

"But he got it right." Raoul shook her gently. "Now that you're here, I'll take you to my grandparents' apartment in the morning. Come on. Much as I'd like to keep you in here all night, I'll drive you back to the *petit château*."

He kept hold of her hand during the quick trip. When he pulled up in front, he took her to the door and unlocked it for her.

"Good night, Abby. I don't dare kiss you again or I'll never leave your apartment. Do you hear what I'm saying?" he ground out with a fierceness that shook her before he disappeared.

Abby awakened early the next morning after a restless night. Today was the day she was going to see something that might be a fantastic new discovery to delight the literary world. But in truth she was still reeling from being in Raoul's arms last night while he'd kissed her senseless.

Everything she'd promised herself not to do, she'd done, like falling in love with him. In his office, he'd pulled her against him and she'd gone willingly, clinging to his tall, hard-muscled body. When he'd picked her up at the train station, she'd known deep down in her bones that she'd wanted to become a part of this man, to merge with him.

Though Ginger and Zoe had told her she'd be taking a risk to go with him, she couldn't help how she was feeling right now. By tonight she would have flown to Venice—far away from his fish bowl—but for the rest of today, she would be with Raoul and it was all she could ask of life.

She debated what to wear to meet his grandparents and finally chose a summery, leaf-green blouse and a green-on-white print skirt. Abby wanted to make a good impression on the relatives he loved.

Her heart jumped when she heard his knock on the entrance door. She hurried across the salon to open it.

To her surprise he wore a dressy black suit with a white shirt and monogrammed tie. Talk about a ducal presence. She couldn't put the image out of her mind. He smelled divine, having just come from the shower, but didn't try to kiss her. His striking looks caused her to stare.

"Raoul—I didn't realize I should get more dressed up."

His gaze traveled over her features. "You look perfect. Shall we go? I'm anxious to be rid of the charlatan image you have of me."

She swallowed hard. "I should never have said it."

One black brow quirked. "If I'd been in your shoes, I'd have said something much worse. Shall we go?"

"Yes."

He closed the door. They walked to his car

and he drove to the château, taking them to the south entrance. "My grandparents live in a suite on the second floor. We won't stay long because they tire easily."

They passed one of the security guards at the door and climbed the marble staircase to the next level. He opened one of the tall paneled double doors and ushered her inside to the main sitting room. A brunette care giver came to greet him.

"Lisette? I'd like you to meet my friend Abby Grant from the United States." He turned to Abby. "Lisette takes care of my grandparents like they were her own parents. She's been with them for two years and we're very lucky to have her."

Abby gave the woman a warm smile. "It's so nice to meet you."

"They're very excited to know Raoul has brought such an important guest. I've taken them into the dining room."

He put a hand on the back of Abby's waist and guided her through another set of French doors to the dining room where his grandparents were waiting for them.

"I bought the latest wheeled chairs that can be used as beds if necessary, so they can be comfortable when there are visitors. Lisette takes impeccable care of them."

"I can see that." Abby could feel his love for them.

The windows looked out on the grounds. Breakfast had been laid out on the round table. There were flowers everywhere.

"What a beautiful room."

"It's their favorite place," Raoul murmured.

"Mon enfant." His silver-haired grandmother lifted her frail arms to him.

His gray-haired grandfather had a harder time and only mouthed his name. He made a hand motion so Raoul would give him a hug.

"Céline and Honoré, I want you to meet the woman I told you about when I called you from Switzerland." Before they'd driven away from the vineyard, he'd let them know he'd fallen in love with her. "This is Abby Grant, the distinguished literature *professeur* from San José, California.

"It's a shame Auguste never got to meet her. She's a kindred spirit, Papi. Because the two of you share a love for Lord Byron's poetry. I wanted her to see the notebook Auguste sent to you."

"It's right here," his grandmother spoke up. "Lisette brought it from the study."

"Why don't you sit by my grandfather, Abby? I'll hand it to you."

After she did his bidding, he reached for it and put the thin, seven-by-three-inch pale blue notebook in her hands.

Her fingers trembled. She looked at his grandfather. "You have no idea what this moment means to me."

"Go ahead and open it," Raoul urged her.

Abby carefully lifted the cover and began studying it. The poem had been written in pencil. "Labyrinths of Lavaux." There it was, just as Raoul had said. She couldn't stop the gasps that kept coming as she read through to the second page, marveling over the poet's thoughts. Like Raoul had told her, it was a short piece, but brilliant. Byron's authentic signature made it priceless.

When she looked up at Raoul, she could hardly make out his features for the tears. "You have a priceless treasure here." She turned to smile at his grandfather. "I'm holding an important part of history in my hand. It's a great honor to be allowed to see this. I can't thank you enough for the privilege."

Honoré nodded with a smile.

Raoul patted the old man's thin shoulder. "Well, Papi, after all these years, you've finally been told by an expert on Lord Byron that this is the treasure you'd always believed it to be."

His grandfather crooked his finger at Abby who gave his hand a squeeze. "I've never been so thrilled, monsieur. This piece on the vineyards must have special significance for you since you ran your own vineyard for fifty years."

The old man nodded.

"Raoul also told me about your dog Vercin-

getorix. Like you, I found Byron's 'Epitaph to a
Dog' very touching. I also loved 'The Prisoner
of Chillon.' Do you know Raoul and I took a
boat ride on the lake right by the château? That's
when he told me about your love for Byron. I
also learned how much he loves his grandparents."

Honoré's eyes misted over and he had enough
strength to smile and press her hand harder.

Raoul leaned down. "Come around and meet
my mamie." Abby moved and sat down next to
his grandmother.

"This is an exciting moment for my husband
and me. I want you to know our Raoul had
his favorite books too." The older woman's soft
brown eyes still twinkled. She looked at her
husband. "Honoré? What one did he love the
most?"

He didn't answer. "My husband has a hard
time talking now."

"That's all right," Abby assured her.

She called to Lisette. "Will you find *Blondine*?
It's in with the old books in the case in the study."

"Bien sûr." While Lisette rushed off, the four of them ate breakfast. Raoul's grandmother only ate a portion of a croissant Abby handed to her. His poor grandfather had to sip a fortified drink through a bent straw. Raoul held it for him.

Lisette came back in the room holding a little tattered storybook. His grandmother took it. "Our Raoul probably hasn't seen this since he was four years old." She had difficulty opening the cover. "Look here. You printed your name the best you could, Raoul. The *u* is upside down." She laughed.

Raoul took the book and showed it to Abby. She looked at it for a minute. Emotions had almost caused her throat to close. His grandmother must have seen how overcome she was. "If you want to keep the book, it's yours, Abby."

"Are you sure?"

She nodded. "Raoul will translate it for you."

"Then I'd love it, Madame," she said in a tremulous voice.

"Call me Céline."

"Thank you, Céline."

Abby listened while Raoul gave them some news about the estate they might enjoy hearing. "Now I can tell you're getting tired, so Abby and I are going to leave. I'm hoping to fit in a drive to Cluny so she can see it."

His grandmother looked at Abby. "The power of the monastery once extended to over ten thousand monks. I was just a girl when I first visited the huge church there, and it made a massive impression on me."

"I'll let you know what I think after we get back, Céline."

"We'll come visit again later, Mamie. Stay well. Love you."

After he hugged them, Abby got up and kissed them on both cheeks. "I'll treasure this book," she whispered to Céline. They said goodbye to Lisette and left the château.

"Your grandparents are very dear," she told him as they walked out to the car.

When he helped her inside, he didn't start it right away. "I don't think I would have made it through this life without them. Do you know when I saw you at the train station, I was reminded of that old French fairy tale you're holding. My grandmother used to read it to me as a child. Have you heard the story of *Blondine*?"

"No."

"'There was a king called Benin. He was good and all the world loved him; he was just, and the wicked feared him. His wife, the Queen Doucette, was also good and much beloved. This happy pair had a daughter called the Princess Blondine, because of her superb golden hair, and she was as amiable and charming as her father the king, and her mother the queen.'

"I loved the beginning of that story, especially the drawings, because their family looked and sounded so happy. I begged my grandmother to read the beginning over and over again. It made me want to crawl inside the pages where I could be that happy too."

Tears stung Abby's eyelids. "Raoul—was your childhood that unhappy?"

"Let's just say it left a lot to be desired. The rest of the fairy tale isn't important. But the picture of Blondine looking so happy stayed with me. That was the look I saw in you that first day, an intangible quality impossible to describe. It's certainly one reason why I was drawn to you."

Listening to Raoul, Abby gained an insight into why he'd told her he didn't want their relationship to cause her pain. His desire to protect her from his difficult family made the kind of sense that helped her to feel closer to him. Combined with his recent loss, it made his desire to crawl into the pages of the fairy tale that much more poignant.

"I had no idea that's what you were thinking about when you got out of that old black car. Thank you for bringing me here to meet your grandparents. I loved seeing Byron's work in his own handwriting. It was a moment I'll never forget. Please know your grandfather's secret is safe with me."

"You're not going to tell your coworkers?"

"Much as I would love to claim I'd come across something of great worth from Byron, in this case it's not my secret to give away, not even to my friends. You told me your grandfather has kept this quiet all these years. It's his secret to keep.

"To be honest, it means much more to me to meet the two people who've had such a great impact on your life."

"As long as you don't think I'm the con artist *par excellence*, I'll sleep better tonight."

"Raoul—" She leaned across the seat and kissed his cheek. "Thank you for today, for everything. I'll cherish these moments and this book forever."

He cupped her face in his hands. "I've done my part, but we haven't talked about your flight to Venice. Have you booked it yet?"

She fought to stifle the pounding of her heart. "No. I didn't know how long we'd be with your grandparents." The thought of leaving him was too painful to consider.

"In that case, would you be willing to attend a funeral service with me first? It starts at noon.

I'd rather not go alone. We'll deal with your flight after."

She couldn't think about leaving right now. "*That's* why you're dressed in black!"

"Yes. It's for one of the estate employees."

Maybe heaven had heard her because she'd been given a reprieve. "After what you've done for me, how could I turn you down?" she answered without hesitation. Besides wanting to be with him, she knew any funeral would be painful for him to get through. If it helped him to be with her, it was the least she could do when he'd given her a gift beyond price.

He kissed her hungrily. "Do you have something black you can wear?"

Abby nodded. "One all-purpose black dress in my small, pitiful wardrobe."

"Then I'll drive you to your apartment and wait while you change."

She slid back to the passenger side, dying inside because he'd been the one to ask her if she'd booked her flight to Italy yet. He'd brought the subject up first. Did it mean he was prepared to let her go? It hit her hard that leaving him was the last thing she wanted to do. Abby was in terrible trouble.

CHAPTER SIX

WHILE RAOUL SAT in his car in front of Abby's apartment, his cell phone rang. His brows furrowed to discover it was his brother. He picked up.

"Jean-Marc?"

"Rumors are that you haven't phoned Solange about tonight's dinner since you got back from Switzerland!" he blurted without preamble.

Raoul's hand tightened around his phone. "Now that you've gotten that off your chest, did you see the text I sent you earlier?"

"I haven't checked my messages."

"Then you need to. Since I'm busy, you and Josette will have to take the parents to the Laroche funeral at the church today. It starts at noon, so plan ahead to make certain father's wheelchair is put close to the front before the priest begins the service. The flowers have been taken care of. *À bientôt.*"

In a few minutes Abby emerged from the *petit château*. At her appearance he drew in a deep breath. The female lines and curves of her figure were made for the simple short-sleeved black dress that fell to her knee. In the darkest room, her hair and eyes would gleam gold and green fire.

He got out to help her into the car. If he didn't suppress the urge to devour her mouth, they would never make it to the funeral. In moments, they headed for the local church.

"Who is the person who passed away?"

"André Laroche. He's been our director of viticulture for sixty years and died at eighty-three. He left a widow, three children and four grandchildren."

"How hard for them. What did he do exactly? That's a long time to carry out one job."

"He managed multiple *terroirs*, a difficult task."

"It's a coveted position, right?"

Raoul nodded.

"I presume there are many others who would like to step into his shoes."

"You have no idea."

"Then you're going to miss him terribly."

Abby had amazing insight *and* compassion. "His sons have helped him, but he's virtually irreplaceable. Still, he has one grandson with a feel for the *terroirs*. Working with his grandfather has helped him to understand climate, soil type and geomorphology. Not everyone is gifted with that sensibility. I have great hopes for him and am grooming him to take over."

"Did André know you wanted his grandson to replace him one day?"

"I assured him of it last month after he'd been put on bed rest for failing kidneys. His heart attack happened after that."

"Oh, the poor thing. But to give him that news was a great compliment and must have thrilled him. You helped him die a happy man."

"You think?"

"I know."

Raoul swallowed hard and clung to her hand. Before long the church came into sight. Already a large crowd had gathered. He found a spot and parked the car. "Stay by me today."

She darted him a puzzled glance. "Where else would I go?"

"One of the relatives might try to take you aside."

"Don't worry," she murmured, giving his hand a reassuring squeeze.

"We'll go in now and pay our respects to his family before the funeral starts."

She held on to his arm as they lined up behind the people and waited their turn to enter the nave. If this hadn't been such a solemn occasion, he would have laughed to see the way every eye in this closed, provincial group of mourners stared at him and Abby.

He saw shock and disbelief in every expression. Angélique had been his *duchesse*-to-be, revered in their elite community. To see him bring another woman to an occasion not meant for outsiders represented something close to blasphemy in their minds. But if he had his way, they were going to have to get used to it.

Raoul walked Abby down the aisle to the front of the chapel, which was filled with flowers. One huge wreath of white roses and lilies with the Decorvet *domaine* banner dominated.

The Laroche family were seated near the draped coffin. Raoul approached André's widow. "Madame Laroche, may I introduce Mademoiselle Grant, visiting from the US? On behalf of the family, I want to tell you how much we'll miss André. He's irreplaceable."

When Abby shook her hand, the other woman broke down. Raoul moved down the line taking Abby with him. He introduced her to each member of the Laroche family. Raoul kept her planted at his side.

Once he'd greeted all of them, he escorted Abby down a side aisle. A fourth of the way, they came to the row where his own family was seated. His graying father sat in the wheelchair on the outside and shot him a black glance of disapproval.

He stopped in front of him. "Papa? Maman? May I present Mademoiselle Grant from San José, California."

His father made no sign of acknowledgment, but his mother said, *"Mademoiselle."*

"It's very nice to meet you," Abby responded.

Next to Raoul's mother sat Josette and her husband, who only nodded. His brother's and sister's judgmental expressions mirrored his parents'.

"Don't forget the dinner tonight," his father half growled at him before they moved on.

Raoul ignored the comment. He was glad he'd brought Abby with him. Now everyone had seen her with him at the same time and they couldn't say a word. He drew her closer and kept walking to the rear where he found them space in the last pew.

Abby sat without moving throughout the service and prayers. Being close to the exit, they were able to leave as soon as the priest gave the final blessing and the pallbearers carried the coffin out to the hearse.

He walked her toward the car. "You can breathe now," he said once they'd gotten inside and had driven away.

"You're not going to the cemetery?"

"No. You and I have provided more than enough interest by being at the funeral. I'll pay my own respects to André when I visit his grave site tomorrow. When I asked you if you'd like to come to France to see Byron's poem, I know you weren't expecting to attend a funeral too."

"Please don't apologize. This is part of who you are."

Again, he reached for her hand. "Is that so?"

"Yes, and you were right about one thing. After we passed your family along the aisle, I found out what it's like to be a fish in a goldfish bowl. What did your father say to you?"

"I have to attend a dinner tonight in Dijon… and I want you to go with me. Tomorrow we'll worry about your flight plans. How do you feel about that?"

She hesitated for a moment. "Is this dinner very important?"

"Not particularly, except that I have to make a few remarks."

"After what you've done for me, of course I'll come."

The blood pounded in his ears. She didn't want to leave him. *He knew it.*

Raoul parked in front of her apartment, determined to grab at happiness for another twenty-four hours. "Do you have something formal to wear for evening?"

"I'm afraid this black dress is it. Why?"

"Since this is the Regional Wine Association Dinner, I thought you might like to visit some of the shops and find something different to wear."

"You don't think black will be appropriate?"

"That question isn't worth answering. But you've already worn it to the funeral and would probably enjoy something different."

"If I had any spending money, there's nothing I'd love more than to buy a new outfit, but my budget won't allow it. When I first flew over, I brought some dressier clothes for the colder weather, but two weeks ago I shipped a lot of them home and kept the black dress to see me through."

"Naturally I intend to buy something that pleases you."

"That's very generous of you. Under the circumstances I'll pick out something to suit the evening."

Afraid he was dreaming, he turned to her. "Hurry inside and get what you need, then we'll drive to Dijon. I'll show you around and then stop to buy you an outfit you can wear right out of the store."

"I'd better bring my black high heel sandals with me."

Unable to hold back another second, he kissed her thoroughly before she left the car. But he was haunted by one question. Did he have the right to love her heart and soul when he hadn't been the kind of husband Angélique had wanted and needed?

Throughout his marriage and after, he'd suffered remorse for not being able to love her. If it was a flaw in him, he hadn't been able to overcome it, even though she'd been the mother of their precious baby.

Could he finally forget the past and embrace the glorious life he wanted with Abby? He could deal with his family's censure, but there was one thing he couldn't endure. That would be to let her get on a plane and fly away. He couldn't let it happen.

Abby had never had so much fun in her life as they spent the rest of the afternoon meandering through the city filled with medieval and renaissance architecture. They would eat a meat pastry here, and a piece of fruit there. Raoul would tease her with a chocolate truffle, then kiss her while they walked on hand in hand.

At five they went to a shop called Clarisse. Abby was afraid to look at the prices. When she found the stunning cherry-red crew neck sheath, she loved it on sight. It had three-quarter sleeves and large colorful flowers on the lower half of the skirt and sleeves. After putting it on with her black heels, she emerged from the dressing room to show Raoul.

The way his black eyes played over her, Abby felt herself to turn to flame. "That's the one."

More than ever she knew this dinner meant something of importance, and she was glad she would be wearing a dress he liked. She gathered her other clothes and they went out to the car.

"Where is the dinner being held?"

"Over at the five-star Grand Hôtel la Cloche. It's been classified as an historic monument overlooking the capital of Burgundy."

In a few minutes, he pointed out the nearby famous Place Darcy. They drove to the private parking before walking inside the hotel to the sumptuous hall with flower-laden banquet tables. At the front of the hall she spotted a rostrum.

Two of the forty or so men and women assembled turned out to be his uncles. Everyone looked elegantly dressed. No wonder Raoul had offered to buy her something special to wear. The seated guests nodded to Raoul while they stared at Abby in what she could only describe as astonishment. After attending the funeral, she ought to be used to it.

"It's already full," she whispered. "Are we late?"

He put his arm around her waist. "It doesn't matter. Now we won't have to wait so long for me to get my part over with. Our place is up in front at the head table."

In seconds, she found herself seated in the middle on Raoul's left. The food had been served and people were starting to drink their wine. He introduced her to a distinguished middle-aged man with a trace of silver in his dark hair on her left. The man couldn't take his eyes off her, but she knew instantly it wasn't because he found her attractive.

"Mademoiselle Grant? I'd like you to meet Monsieur Raimund Godard, owner of the prestigious Pascal Godard Domaine here in Burgundy," Raoul spoke in English. "And on his left, his daughter Solange."

Abby smiled. "How do you do, Monsieur, Mademoiselle?" She assumed his daughter wasn't married since Raoul hadn't attached a different last name to her.

"Mademoiselle Grant," the man murmured.

The other woman leaned forward to see around her father. Abby had heard the expression "staring daggers" at someone. She now saw it for herself. Solange de la Croix Godard, a real beauty with copper-red hair sweeping her shoulders, came close to impaling Abby with the dark brown eyes she'd inherited from her father.

By now Raoul had gotten involved in a conversation with an older man seated on his right. Abby ate in silence until another man, seated at the end of the table, walked up to the rostrum. He tapped his wineglass with a fork to get everyone's attention and introduced himself. After a welcoming speech in French, he asked Raoul to come up.

"I won't be long," he whispered against her ear before he made his way to the podium. She was still reacting to the contact when he started speaking. Throughout the five-minute speech she didn't understand, she sensed Solange's eyes on her, but Abby refused to let her know she was aware of her.

There was a burst of applause before Raoul returned to the table. Two other men gave speeches and dessert was served. Raoul put an arm around the back of her chair. "If you're ready, we'll leave now."

That was fine with Abby, who didn't like being the center of attention. He held her chair while she got up, and then the two of them left the banquet hall, aware every eye had followed them out of the room.

"There. That wasn't so bad."

She gave an ironic chuckle, but didn't say anything as he helped her into the car. When he got behind the wheel, Abby turned to him. "What was your speech about? You got a resounding ovation."

"Remember when I told you that France's grape harvest was among the smallest in thirty years, down ten percent from the year before?"

She nodded. "I passed on some thoughts my grandfather and I discussed recently. It's still too early to draw a conclusion about the quality of the wine this year. In truth, the future weather conditions haven't been predicted by the experts to be all that bad even if the quantity of the wine will be economically tight.

"That's why it's advisable for some vineyards that have a system of reserves to hold back selling a part of the production year to year. That practice serves as insurance to help ride out those times when there is a poor grape harvest."

"That's what you've been doing on your estate?"

"And will continue to do. My grandfather and I are in lockstep on that score, even if some of the family have a hard time wanting to conserve," he emphasized.

"I'm sure that's why you're in charge."

"Many of my family members would like to replace me if it weren't Decorvet tradition that the eldest son becomes head of the estate if the present owner dies or is unable to function."

"What about the eldest female if she's the oldest sibling?"

"Not in my archaic family, even if she's the most qualified."

"That leaves your sister out. How does she feel about it?"

"I'll leave that to your imagination."

"For what it's worth, I think your family is lucky with you at the helm. Thanks to you they still have their legacy and have survived, even after passing through such a terrible harvest."

He flicked her a burning glance. "I can't wait to get you home."

The impact of those words sent a thrill through her body. "Raoul—the daughter of the man I sat next to tonight, Solange, kept staring at me with hostile eyes. I'm not making it up."

"I know you're not."

Abby struggled to find the right words. "I can only assume she wished she'd been with you tonight."

They left the hotel for home. "One of these days she'll find the right man."

But Solange wanted Raoul.

"What's going on in your mind?"

"Nothing specific." Which wasn't true.

"That's the first lie you've told me. Tell me what's bothering you.

"Was it accidental that we sat right next to the Godard family?"

"No. The Wine Association plans these regional dinners and they always place the head *domaine* owners at the same table. It's a tradition I'd love to see abolished, but it's not my decision."

Abby noticed they were headed back to the estate. "Solange's father gave off an unsettling aura of hostility too."

"He's hoping I'll propose to her. There's nothing he'd rather see than a marriage between his *domaine* and ours. I knew which way the wind was blowing a year ago. That's why he brought her to the dinner tonight. When you and I sat down at the table, he came close to having a coronary."

"Good heavens—" she cried. "Does everyone have an agenda?"

"Not my grandparents. After we reach the cottage, I'll explain my reasons."

Her breath caught. "Do you think that's a good idea?"

His face closed up. "The entire region is aware that there's a new woman in my life. An American woman no less, one who knows nothing about vineyards and doesn't speak French except for a few words like *absolument, chasselas* and *Saint des Saints*."

She lowered her head.

"Now that I've gotten my duties out of the way, I'm planning to concentrate on you. You're the only thing of real importance to me. I don't want to waste a moment of our precious time together."

"But to go to your private home—"

"Abby—it must have occurred to you by now that I don't want you to leave." He reached for her hand and kissed the palm. The gesture melted her to the core.

"Surely you realize I'm asking you to spend the night with me. I've wanted you from the very first moment we met." *I've wanted you too, Raoul.* "I need to feel you in my arms and hold you. But if you don't feel that way about me, then I don't want you to be uncomfortable. All you have to do is tell me."

Abby was listening. He was the most honorable man she'd ever known. The way his marriage had ended so cruelly had left him grief stricken and she understood his needs.

She had needs too. Abby knew deep in her soul that Raoul would always be the great love of her life. If she gave in to her desires for a night of temporary rapture, it would ruin her for other men. To go back to California and pine for Raoul for the rest of her life was unthinkable. She couldn't put herself through that kind of hell.

Don't let it go any further, Abby.

She didn't dare bring that unending pain on herself. It was going to be like a death to fly to

Venice tomorrow, but she knew it was what she had to do for self-preservation.

"I think you'd better drive me to the guest apartment."

Without his saying a word, he drove her to the *petit château*. He helped her with her things and walked her to her apartment where he set everything down. His dark eyes narrowed on her mouth. She could almost feel him kissing her.

"Go ahead and make plane arrangements. I'll call you in the morning. Depending on the time of your flight, I'll pick you up for breakfast in the morning and drive you to the airport."

"Wait—" she cried because he'd pivoted too fast and was already walking away.

He looked over his shoulder. "That wouldn't be a good idea."

When she couldn't hear his car, she shut the door, devastated by what had just happened. She waited there for at least five minutes, hoping he'd come back and beg her to reconsider. But it was evident it wasn't going to happen.

If he'd really wanted to be with her tonight, he would have found a way.

She hurried in the bedroom to call the girls. Though it was late, she had to talk to them. She phoned Zoe first and got her voice mail. Too frustrated to leave a message, she called Ginger.

"Abby? Hey—what are you doing phoning this late?"

"I'm sorry, but I'm flying to Venice tomorrow and will try to plan a flight that fits in with yours and Zoe's schedule."

"You're not staying in Burgundy?"

A shuddering sigh escaped. "No."

"So the 'come and see my notebook' thing turned out not to be for real."

She gripped her phone so tightly, she could have crushed it. "Actually there was a notebook with a poem, but it wasn't an authentic signature of Byron's." In this instance, she had to lie after promising Raoul she'd let the find stay a secret.

"But he really had something to show you?"

"Yes. I met his grandparents and they showed it to me."

"Then he was on the level."

"Yes."

"You sound odd. Are you okay? What's going on with you two?"

"It's been a very full day with a funeral and a dinner. He's a very important man." But to-night he hadn't pressured her to stay with him and it hurt like crazy.

"Don't let me keep you up any longer. Shall I come early or late? You'd better check with Zoe."

"She's not here."

"What do you mean?"

"Zoe decided to fly to Greece early, so I took her to the airport today and now I have the car. Tomorrow is Sunday and I'm going to Burano Island for a couple of days. I've already paid for travel and the hotel room for two nights on a special deal. Why don't you check flights for Tuesday and I'll meet you whenever you say?"

Another two days with Raoul. Abby could hardly breathe.

"That sounds fine. I'll call you Tuesday and we'll plan from there."

"Perfect."

CHAPTER SEVEN

AT SIX-THIRTY SUNDAY MORNING, Raoul's phone awakened him. He worried it might be Abby and checked the caller ID. One look and he knew his father was summoning him, but he ignored it.

Last night he'd worked for a half hour sending instructions to Félix, then he'd stretched out on the couch in his office. It had taken all the self-control he could muster to leave Abby alone.

The phone rang again. Raoul got to his feet and clicked it on. *"Bonjour, Papa. Ça va bien?"*

"You and I need to talk." His father never changed.

"Whatever it is, let's do it on the phone now. I have other business in a little while." Like driving Abby to the airport.

"You're talking about that American woman

staying at the *petit château* who is out for all she can get. Jean-Marc told me you met her in St. Saphorin. Whatever possessed you to bring her here?"

"With the property sold, she and her friends didn't feel right about staying on the vineyard for their vacation. I invited them to come here for a few days."

"But only one arrived with you. How dare you take her to the funeral! It shocked everyone to see you with someone else so soon after Angélique's death."

So soon? After two years? Raoul had to count to ten.

"I heard you took her to the banquet last night. Solange expected you to take her."

"I'm not interested in Solange and never will be. Abby has never been to France and I wanted to be a good host."

"She's not one of us," his father muttered angrily. "It would never do for you to form an attachment. You must see that! I want you to get rid of her."

Raoul grimaced because part of what his father said kept his guilt alive. "Was there something important about vineyard business you needed to discuss with me?"

"How soon is she leaving?"

"I have no idea." That much was the truth at least.

"You can't allow this to go on. Your mother and sister won't stand for it and I forbid it! The whole family is in an uproar. Pierre rang me when he got home from the banquet, demanding to know how she managed to be at the head table. If you don't cut her loose, I'll cut you out of the family business."

It didn't surprise him that his father would go that far. Again, Raoul chose to ignore it. "How are you feeling today?"

"How do you think?

"I've made arrangements for Dr. Filbert to be by later to check on you and the grandparents. He'll give me an update on your condition."

"The only thing I want you to do is make sure she's gone by tonight."

Click.

He didn't like that his father was in pain and suffered, but since the crash, Raoul hadn't let anyone dictate what he'd do with his life. After setting the electronic lock, he drove back to the cottage for a shower and shave. Then he made the phone call to Abby, prepared to tell her he didn't want her to leave.

"Raoul," she answered on the second ring. "I'm glad you called. There's been a change in plans with my friends. I won't be able to meet up with Ginger until Tuesday, but I'll book my flight for tomorrow around noon."

"If she's not going to be there until Tuesday, then you and I should make the most of the time."

"I… I'm afraid it's just prolonging the inevitable," her voice faltered.

"I never want you to leave, so don't pretend otherwise." When his heart rate slowed down he said, "If you're ready, I'll come by for you now, and take you to breakfast. I don't know about you, but I'm hungry."

"All right." Her quiet response was all he needed to hear.

After hanging up, he hardly remembered getting in the Maserati to drive to her apartment. She was out in front when he drove up. Those jewel-green eyes were the first thing he saw. Raoul sensed Abby was anxious, but she looked a vision in jeans and the same white-on-black print top she'd been wearing the day they met.

"Bonjour, ma belle."

"Good morning," came her slightly breathless greeting. While her glazed eyes played over him, a little vein throbbed at the base of her throat.

"I thought about you all night." Heat swept into her cheeks. He walked her to the car, holding on to her arm. "Are you hungry?"

"I think by now you know you don't ever have to ask me that question."

He gave her a kiss on the cheek after helping her into the passenger seat. "I'm hoping you'll enjoy La Mère Valois. It serves a simple breakfast eaten by the locals. Homemade country-style bread fresh from the oven and hot coffee."

"Mmm. A totally French breakfast."

"*Oui.* They have yogurt and fresh fruit if you ask for it."

"I'll have what you have."

"I'm warning you now I follow a Spartan diet in the morning."

Five minutes later he'd taken her inside the little bistro and had shown her how to dip her bread into the coffee and eat it. She followed his lead and probably disliked it, but she pretended to enjoy it.

"You're sure you don't want anything else?"

Her eyes flashed. "Positive. As long as I'm in France you know…"

Abby's spirit of adventure prompted her to try anything. She had many qualities he was crazy about. "I'll feed you properly after we reach Cluny."

When they'd finished eating, he walked her out to the car and helped her in. "We're supposed to get a fair amount of sun today." He'd left the top down.

"Is Cluny far?"

"Sixty miles. Long enough for you to tell me what's going on with your friends."

"Zoe decided to leave for Greece early, and Ginger has already made plans away from Venice for a few days."

"Does that upset you?"

"You don't really expect me to answer that question."

"We're together for a while longer. I can't ask for more than that right now."

She looked around. "The scent of the flowers is heavenly here, Raoul."

"Pollination is going on everywhere."

"You tried to embarrass me once, but you won't succeed again."

"I have to make one stop at the cemetery, then we'll leave for Cluny."

Elation to be with Abby filled his system as he drove beyond the church to the place where André had been buried. Floral arrangements still decorated the grave site. Two figures were huddled there. Raoul stopped the car. "I won't be long."

Abby watched him walk over to the man and woman and kiss them on both cheeks. He must have wanted to be alone with them.

She reached into her purse and pulled out the little storybook his grandmother had given her. There was something touching about seeing Raoul's name printed by him at such a young age.

It thrilled her that his grandmother had kept his favorite book all these years. No doubt she'd realized early on how much Raoul needed to be with them. She wiped her eyes when she realized he hadn't had that same relationship with his own parents.

She'd been broken up after the visit to his grandparents and had needed a good cry. Their sweetness explained more than anything else why he adored them. The love between the three of them and the way he cared for them was moving beyond words.

Abby understood a few of the French words as she turned the scant pages. The artist had created a dreamy rendition of Blondine. In the story, she wore her golden hair long, like Abby had done before getting hers cut. But whatever likeness Raoul saw between Blondine and Abby had to exist in his mind because they were nothing alike. The idea that Abby was dreamy-looking would never have occurred to her.

She held the book and reflected on the talk with Ginger last night. While she thought about the way everything had changed since they'd all met in Switzerland, Raoul returned to the car. He eyed the book.

"My grandmother would never have given it to you if she didn't know you'd appreciate it."

Abby took a shuddering breath. "How much do they know about us?" she asked before putting it away.

"I rang them from Switzerland before we left

La Floraison and told them I'd met a woman who had already changed my life."

Raoul, her heart cried. So *that* was the reason she'd given the book to Abby. She couldn't believe he'd shared something so personal with them before bringing her to France. "They… were wonderful and accepting in a way I can't describe."

"That's who they are. Looking at them yesterday made me realize their time is short."

She put the book back in her purse. Abby had yet to contact her own parents and tell them she wasn't with the girls, that she'd driven to France with a stranger and was out of her mind in love.

"I take it you were speaking to some of André's relatives."

"His grandson and wife. He fears he doesn't have what it takes to fill his grandfather's shoes. I've said what I can to reassure him."

"Wait and see. Knowing how you feel about him will go a long way to helping him, Raoul."

"One can hope."

"You have a way with people or they wouldn't

revere you so highly. Once in a while you should accept a compliment. Or doesn't mine count?"

"More than you know. But as you've discovered, I've brought you to a hornet's nest."

"Except you can't say that about your grandparents. They adore you and I can see why they mean so much to you. But it hurts me for your sake that you and your parents don't have the same relationship."

"*Papa* wants things from me I can no longer give him."

"Like what?"

"He's expecting me to marry Solange."

"But that doesn't make sense."

"I know, but you try telling my father."

"Has he ever been happy?" she asked.

"Yes. When I married Angélique."

"So Solange is second best."

"He believes she will fill the role adequately."

Abby shook her head. "I'll never understand that kind of thinking."

"I didn't understand it from the cradle."

They left the cemetery behind. Once out on

the open road they passed one charming village after another. Abby loved the scented breeze that ruffled their hair. With a disheveled look, Raoul was almost too breathtaking.

But this wasn't like the carefree drive they'd taken from Switzerland to Burgundy. Her whole body and soul ached for the love of this unique man who exuded a melancholy brought on by many things.

When they reached Cluny, they parked and walked around the monastery where there were crowds of tourists. Raoul wasn't in a mood to talk except to make a few comments about its history. For once he didn't reach for her hand. Not only the physical, but the mental separation was killing her. She took a few pictures of Raoul along with the abbey, then put her phone away.

"Are you ready to go back?"

She nodded and they walked to his car. Once he'd helped her inside, he asked her where she would like to eat. "Can we do what we did at the border? Buy some picnic food and eat it in the car on the way home?"

Without saying a word, he drove to an *épicerie* where they bought a small feast of finger foods and drinks. Then they were off again. The silence tore her apart. By the time they returned to the estate and he parked in front of the *petit château*, she was worried about him but didn't know how to help him.

For once he didn't get out of the car. He didn't plan to walk her to the door.

"Raoul? Would you come in with me?"

His eyes were slits when he looked at her. "I think not, and you know why."

"Please. I know something has been bothering you, but we can't talk about it out here where people will see us."

After a long wait he unbent enough to get out of the car. He followed her in and shut the apartment door.

"Why don't you freshen up in the guest bathroom before we talk?"

While he did her bidding, she visited her own

en suite bathroom and returned to the salon. He was already back and on the phone. The grimace on his face was chilling. A minute later he hung up. Their gazes collided.

"Is everything all right?"

"No. Pierre has had another blowup over a bad decision Jean-Marc made with a client about lowering prices. It's the second time he's done it. Pierre's gone to my father about it and there's going to be hell to pay."

"Do you need to be there?"

"Yes. I'll tell my father what I think should be done, but he'll fight me on it like he always does."

"I thought you were the head of the *domaine*."

"He may be living inside a crippled, arthritic body, but there's nothing wrong with his mind. My father's a raging anachronism, still believing in the divine right of dukes. He resents his disability."

"So he takes it out on you. What was his excuse before he was afflicted?"

Raoul rubbed the back of his neck. She doubted he'd ever been asked that question before. "That my grandfather was still looked to as the true head."

"And now it's the way everyone looks to you." They stared at each other. "You rarely talk about your mother."

"She's lives for my father and what he decides. If she's ever defied him, I don't remember it. I'm sure she loves me and my siblings in her own way, but it has always been clear our father came first with her. I learned early that trying to appeal to her for something that went against my father's wishes fell on deaf ears."

On that note he started for the door. "We'll have to talk later. I don't know how long this will take, but I'll call you."

She followed him. "I'll find a way to stay busy."

He left without kissing her. Since leaving the cemetery his behavior had changed. For the time being she was helpless to do anything about it.

* * *

Raoul left her apartment and drove to the château. His parents' suite was on the second floor in the opposite wing from his grandparents.

"Maman." He kissed her cheek after entering their salon.

"Now that you've come, I'll be in the garden."

Maman was too thin, but with her strawberry blond hair and fine features, she was still attractive. He watched her leave the room like the good wife his father had trained her to be. Jean-Marc stood near the fireplace with a foul expression on his face.

Their uncle Pierre, filled with resentment to have to be in this situation at all, sat in a chair across from their father whose wheelchair had been rolled in. He couldn't manage it alone. Josette and Paul sat on the couch.

Raoul lounged against the wall and looked at his father. "What is it you want to say?"

"Jean-Marc has undermined Pierre twice on prices to foreign buyers."

"Because they're too high!" his brother argued. In principle he was right, but the Vosne-Romanée wine region would always demand the highest prices.

"Did you hear that?" his father almost shouted. "This can't go on. I won't allow it. You said you had an idea."

His father wouldn't be happy, but Raoul had to try for all their sakes. "Forget what's happened in the past. Jean-Marc has always been very good with people. He knows how to handle them. If you want my opinion, he should be working where he can do the most good."

With that remark, surprise broke out on his brother's face.

"Go on," his father barked.

"Pierre and Grégoire see eye to eye. Why not let father and son work together from now on? I'd like to pull Jean-Marc from the exporting department and give him a new position that's been needed for a long time."

"What do you mean?" His father always seemed to growl.

"For want of a better word, let him be the concierge of the estate with an office in the main building of the *domaine*. We've never had an official one, but I believe it's time to make some important changes. We need someone to meet and greet, to act as a liaison for all the different aspects of the business."

"That's part of your job as CEO," he fired at Raoul.

"When you can find me." He shook his head. "I have other concerns to do with our investments that require my full attention these days. Jean-Marc and I learned the business from you. No one knows more about our history than he does. He'd be our most valuable asset."

For once his father didn't have a comeback.

"I recommend that he and Grégoire start their new jobs today. Then everyone should be happy. Now you'll all have to excuse me."

"Where are you going?"

He glanced at his brother-in-law. "I was hoping to have a business conference with Paul. Are you free now?"

Paul eyed him in surprise. "Of course."

"Good. Then I'll leave it to you to sort everything else out, Papa."

"I want an answer to a question before you go. How soon will the American be leaving?"

His father couldn't resist. "You asked me that before. Remember she and her friends were cheated out of their vacation in Switzerland because Auguste's estate had to be sold. She's still not through sightseeing." How he enjoyed saying that. *"À bientôt."*

He left the room with Paul and they drove away from the château.

Abby had no idea how long Raoul would be. Since she had the afternoon ahead of her, she decided to go for a walk through the vineyards.

The sky had darkened by the time she stepped outside moments later. Not used to the climate yet, she couldn't tell if it might rain later. Maybe she wouldn't be able to explore for as long, but it didn't matter. She started out on the main road, then took a different road to the left. The workers were already out. Some waved to her and she waved back.

Every so often she passed little huts or shacks. There were a couple of men in pants and work shirts talking outside the third one. They eyed her with unmistakable male interest.

"Eh, bien. Mademoiselle Grant."

"Oh—Jean-Marc!"

He turned to the other man who seemed close to his age. "Gilles? This is the *Americaine* I was telling you about who's visiting the *domaine*."

The other guy flashed her a smile. "You're the one from California." He spoke with a heavy French accent. "I saw you with Raoul at the dinner last night."

She nodded. "He thought I'd enjoy seeing what goes on in the world of a vintner."

His eyes squinted at her. "How do you like it so far?"

"I'm still trying to take it all in."

Gilles smiled. "I'd be happy to show you more after work."

With that comment, Jean-Marc moved closer

to her. "I'm free now and will do the honors. We'll talk later, Gilles. *À bientôt.*"

Abby hadn't expected to run into Jean-Marc. "I don't want to interrupt your work."

His beguiling smile was reminiscent of Raoul's. "I've just been made the new concierge for the estate. Since this *is* my work now, visitors are our first priority."

"Well, thank you."

So their father *had* listened to Raoul and now his brother had been given a position of importance. His compassion, even in the midst of turmoil, made Abby love him all the more.

"It's going to rain soon. I'll accompany you to the main *domaine* building. In my private office you'll see some ancient maps of our ducal land dating from the fifteenth century."

Abby assumed it might have been an office Raoul had used and had just relinquished in order to keep the peace.

"I'm a history buff and would love to see those."

His dark brows lifted. "What do you do when you're not traveling?"

"I'm a teacher of early nineteenth-century romance poets and writers at San José State University. My classes start again in the fall."

They started walking back to the main road. He cocked his head. "Even if you are on vacation, there must be a man in your life." Her heart jumped. *Only one.* "Is he anxiously awaiting your return?"

"Why do you ask?"

"Because if there is no one, I would like very much to get to know you better while you're here. Not long ago Raoul buried his heart with his wife and daughter. What you wouldn't know is that Solange de la Croix Godard, the woman you would have met at the dinner, is waiting for him to come out of his mourning period so they can be married."

Abby was aghast that Jean-Marc would warn her off his own brother that way when he knew nothing about their relationship. "I heard about their deaths" was all she said in a quiet tone.

They came to the *domaine*'s headquarters where half a dozen cars were parked. He took her inside, introducing her to several people working in the different offices, among them Félix Moirot, Raoul's sandy haired private secretary.

"Come with me." Jean-Marc showed her inside a huge office that was more like a museum. The maps and charts of the estate with its hectares of vines on every wall, all under glass, fascinated her. "You start in that corner. By the time you've made a tour of the whole room, you'll have seen the entire Decorvet chronological history."

"I've never seen anything like this!"

"I'm not surprised Raoul hasn't shown it to you. He has too many calls on his time."

"I'm sure that's true," she murmured.

The less they talked about him the better. "Do you mind if I study these for a little while?"

"Be my guest."

He stayed at the desk to make phone calls, leaving her to examine the earliest wall hanging. It was a charter with the ducal insignia of a lion, just like the one on the gate at the entrance to the estate. The handmade drawing showed two *terroirs*, intricate and incredible.

The rain pounded on the roof as she moved around the room, examining each step of history. Abby marveled at the artwork. The wording of the earlier drawings was done in old French. But her heart was heavy. Raoul had said he didn't want their relationship blighted by his complicated family. Jean-Marc had done a good job of putting a damper on this day.

He eventually walked over to her. His dark eyes were smiling. "I never saw anyone take this kind of time to look at everything." It sounded like a genuine compliment He was quite attractive in his own way. Abby felt sorry for him. To live in Raoul's unmatchable shadow wouldn't have been easy.

"Only a few people in the world have a heritage like yours. It's wonderful and different from anything I've ever known. I'm grateful you've let me browse to my heart's content."

"Grateful enough to let me take you for an early dinner? The rain has stopped and I need to eat."

It was getting late. Already ten to five. Abby had to do some quick thinking. She hadn't heard from Raoul, and she was hungry too. Why not agree with him so he wouldn't know his remarks had gotten under her skin?

"I'd enjoy that as long as it's close to the estate and doesn't keep you from your work too long."

He shook his head. "Entertaining a guest is part of the job, especially one as attractive as you."

Oh, dear. "Thank you. You make a great tour director." The remark was meant to put him off any ideas he had.

He led her out of the office to a silver Mercedes and unlocked it with a remote. The parking area still had puddles from the rain. She hurried to get in before he could help her, already fearing this wasn't a good idea.

To her relief he drove them to a small bistro in the village called Le Petit Pinot Noir. She pronounced the name out loud, loving the sound of it. When he asked her why she chuckled at the sight of it, she said, "I think it's a very clever name."

Again, she got out before he could come around and went into the restaurant first. Jean-Marc found a table by the window and gave their order to the waitress. "I've ordered us *boeuf bourguignon*, a regional favorite."

"That sounds good."

He ordered a bottle of red wine and poured some for her. "Try this, then later tonight I'll take you to our wine cellars where you can taste our superior *cru*."

"I did have some at the dinner last night. I'm no connoisseur, but it was like velvet."

"But they didn't serve you from a fifteen-year-old bottle. *That's* an experience." His eyes traveled over her while he drank his wine. She hadn't changed her mind about him. He was a flirt. She would simply have to see this through.

Within minutes the waitress arrived with their meal. The meat had been cooked in wine with baby onions and mushrooms. What made the difference in the flavor were the little bits of bacon. "This is delicious."

"I thought you'd like it."

When she lifted her head to smile, a gasp escaped her lips and every thought went out of her head. Raoul, dressed in a polo shirt and chinos, had just entered the bistro with another man who was dark-blond and looked to be in his mid-thirties. Then she remembered seeing him at the funeral. It was Paul. He'd been the one sitting next to Raoul's sister.

Raoul's black gaze surveyed the room, looking for a free table when he zeroed in on Abby. Lines darkened his features to see that she was with his brother. He walked over to them without hesitation and drew up two chairs.

"So this is where you are. Mind if we join you?" he asked, staring directly at her.

CHAPTER EIGHT

ABBY WAS SO happy to see him she blurted, "I'm glad you've come!"

The waitress came over and took their orders.

"Abby? You met our brother-in-law, Paul Ridoux, at the funeral. He's married to Josette."

"Hello again."

"Have you enjoyed your day so far?" Raoul inquired as if they were the only ones at the table.

"Very much because I've learned a lot. While I was out walking in the vineyard, I met your cousin Gilles and your brother. He took me to the *domaine* office so I could see all the maps. I'm afraid I studied them too long."

"You liked the display?" His eyes seemed to pierce hers.

"Who wouldn't? But a lot of the script was in

Old French. I would imagine that would take a long time to learn."

"Not if the interest is there."

What did he mean by that? "Do you know this bistro has the funniest name? The Petit Pinot Noir has a ring to it that makes me laugh."

"I can't figure out why," Jean-Marc interjected.

But Raoul could. Suddenly she saw amusement light up his eyes, melting the frost.

Had he been upset because she'd come with his brother? Raoul had given her a look she never wanted to see again. When she got him alone, she'd explain the circumstances.

Soon their meal arrived and the waitress brought two more wineglasses. Raoul reached for the bottle and filled three of the goblets. The other one was Abby's, but she'd barely touched hers.

"Let's drink in celebration. The *domaine* has a new concierge in Jean-Marc, and Paul has just accepted the management of our European investment accounts." When their father died,

Raoul would make Josette the head of the company. "My workload has just been cut in half and no one could be happier than I am. Next week we'll fly to Paris, Paul, and I'll introduce you to the groups I've been working with."

"I'll look forward to that."

Abby rarely drank alcohol, but this was one time she felt she needed it and picked up her glass to sip some. After they ate, Raoul was the first to break up their meal. He put some bills on the table that covered everyone's food and got to his feet.

"We've all got more work to do before this day is out. Since I have to run Paul back to the château, I'll take you with us, Abby."

Thank heaven he'd said that.

He looked at his brother. "That'll free you to meet the Spanish *ambassadeur* from Madrid. Félix just informed me that he and his entourage will be arriving within ten minutes. I have no doubts you'll have them eating out of your hand." He eyed Abby. "Shall we go?"

She stood up. "Thank you so much for the

tour, Jean-Marc. It's been one of the highlights of my trip here. And this is a charming little bistro."

"À tout moment," he said through wooden lips.

Abby didn't know what that meant. But she did know that the advent of Raoul coming into the restaurant had changed Jean-Marc's mood and she couldn't have been more grateful to leave.

When they walked out to the Jaguar, Paul climbed in back and Raoul helped her in the front passenger seat. On the short drive back to the estate, she turned to him. "I've never heard the expression *à tout moment.*"

"My brother meant that he would be glad to do it for you anytime."

"Oh. Thanks for telling me." She looked over her shoulder at Paul. "I understand you and your wife have one child and another one on the way."

He nodded. "Maurice is three and waiting for a brother."

"How exciting! When's the due date?"

"Two months."

"Have you thought of a name yet?'

"No. We're still arguing over it."

She smiled, but talk of babies was no doubt painful to Raoul. If he married again and had a child, would it help fill the hole in his heart? Every day he had to live with the loss of his little girl.

Before long they arrived at the estate. Raoul stopped at the *petit château* and let her out. "I'll call you in a few minutes."

She nodded. "It was nice talking with you Paul." Abby got out of the car and hurried inside her apartment, wishing Raoul didn't have to leave.

Much as Raoul wanted to follow her, he had to drop Paul off first.

His brother-in-law leaned forward. "She's one beautiful woman. Nice."

"I agree. If we hadn't happened to stop in

there, Jean-Marc would have forgotten all about the appointment with the Spanish contingent."

Except that it wasn't an accident. Raoul had seen Jean-Marc's car. He was curious why he'd gone there to eat so late on his first day as concierge. It wasn't his kind of place. Seeing Abby at the table explained everything.

Raoul wound around to the east entrance. Paul got out. "I can't thank you enough for giving me the new job. I know Josette complained to your father."

"That's not the reason, Paul. Since my trip to Switzerland, I've been thinking about several changes to relieve me of so much work. Your head for finance makes you the ideal choice to work with the Paris group. You'll be a great asset."

"Thanks for the confidence, Raoul."

They shook hands. After he walked away, Raoul headed back to Abby's apartment. He phoned her from the car to let her know he was out in front. She didn't know it yet, but he had plans for the two of them.

She came out the entrance a minute later and hurried to the car. After she got inside she said, "I hope you don't thin—"

"I don't think anything," he cut her off. "Jean-Marc has always had a roving eye."

"Still, you looked upset when you first walked into the bistro, and I couldn't explain. The thing is, I didn't know what to do when Jean-Marc saw me out in the vineyard and told me he would show me the office. I didn't want to be rude to him."

"Rudeness isn't in your nature. What you saw was a man who experienced a temporary fit of jealousy when he saw you having dinner with another man, even if he happened to be his own brother."

His admission thrilled her. "Thanks to you he's very happy about his new position."

"I'm glad to hear it."

"Your brother-in-law must be happy too."

"I believe he is. Before I let Paul out, you should know he said you're beautiful. In private he said he could understand Jean-Marc's interest. The whole estate is talking about you."

"What an exaggeration."

"You think? Paul and I had to stop by the *domaine* office. Every male there mentioned he'd gone off with the stunning blonde *Americaine*. Gilles happened to be there and was upset because he'd planned to ask you out for dinner after work, but Jean-Marc got there first."

"I'd rather not talk about that. Where are we going?"

"Where we won't be disturbed."

Her breath caught as he drove them along several roads that wound deep into the vineyard. Raoul had told her before that there were only two places where they could be together in private. Since he wasn't taking her to his office at the château, there was only one other spot she could think of.

When they came to a low-lying ridge, she saw a charming cottage straight out of a Grimm's fairy tale. Raoul hadn't exaggerated about where he lived. From the massive Decorvet château to this isolated hideaway?

As they drew closer she noticed his Maserati parked around the side. He pulled to a stop in front and turned off the engine.

"I wish you hadn't brought me here." Her desire to be alone with him was like a flash fire. She no longer felt she had the strength to keep him at a distance. If she went inside with him, she'd become the wanton who lived only for him.

"I want to discuss something important with you. Surely you're not afraid of me. Have I ever taken advantage of you?"

"You don't have to," she admitted. Abby despised her own weakness.

"Since providence has given us until tomorrow before you have to leave, it seems fate has chosen the moment to be now."

"What moment?"

"I'm afraid you don't know what you awakened when you were willing to come to Bur-

198 CAPTIVATED BY THE BROODING BILLIONAIRE

gundy with me. You're familiar with the saying, 'who rides the tiger'?"

"Of course."

"Then you understand my meaning."

He was being cryptic. But before she could ask for an explanation, Raoul helped her out of the car and walked her inside.

After turning on a lamp, he showed her around the modernized, comfortable-looking interior. The small cottage contained a living room and a kitchen off to the side. There were two bedrooms and a bathroom.

But all Abby could see were the small framed pictures on his bedroom dresser. One showed his lovely wife holding the baby. The rest were photos of his little daughter, Nicolette. Jean-Marc's words pressed in on her.

Not long ago Raoul buried his heart with his wife and daughter.

He handed her one so she could see it up close. "Oh, Raoul—she's adorable and had your black hair."

"She had colic and cried a lot in the beginning. I walked the floor with her many a night."

Tears filled her eyes. "I can only imagine your pain."

"It never leaves, but the initial, excruciating pain has gone. Now it's more a case of what happens when I see any young child My mind immediately imagines my little daughter at that age, probably following Maurice around."

"I'm sure I would do the same thing for the rest of my life."

She put the picture back and left the bedroom. He followed her into the living and grasped her around the waist from behind, burying his face in her hair.

"I've learned to live with it." But had he? "What I'm waiting to hear is your impression of my private *Saint des Saints*."

She turned in his arms. "It's cozy and warm. You'd never know that the most famous vintner in all Burgundy hides out in here instead of the château you call a relic."

His white smile turned her heart over in the

semidarkness of the room. "Do you like it enough to stay here with me tonight? Now that I have you to myself, I have no cares."

"I thought you brought me here to talk."

"Later."

He pressed a hungry kiss to her mouth, tasting it over and over again. This was what she'd been aching for all day. Too soon they were both breathless. Raoul was the most beautiful, virile man she'd ever seen in her life. In her heart she knew his first wife had to have felt the same way about him.

Had they made love before their marriage? No woman could ever be immune to him, and he would have felt some attraction to Angélique or he couldn't have married her.

Did she dare dream that Raoul would ask Abby to marry him? She didn't have to hear Jean-Marc's warning again that Raoul had buried his heart at the funeral. If he'd been letting her know marriage to Raoul wasn't in Abby's destiny, he'd done a good job. She tore her lips from his.

"Raoul—we shouldn't be doing this. I'll be leaving in a few days."

He shook his head. "I can't let you go. Let me love you, *mon amour*. While we were in Switzerland, my soul was struck by what we French call the *coup de foudre*. Love at first sight. It makes no sense, but there's no other explanation to account for my feelings since I met you. Don't be nervous."

"But I am," she confessed in a tremulous voice.

"Why? I know you want this too."

"I do. More than anything I've ever wanted in my life, but we're not thinking clearly. There are too many reasons why we mustn't."

He crushed her against him. "Name one that matters."

"How do we know this *coup de foudre* won't happen to you again?"

"You mean to *us*! No, *mon amour*, you and I have experienced something that only happens once in a lifetime."

"But your family needs more time."

Raoul released her enough to look at her with a puzzled expression. "What's going on with you? My family has nothing to do with my personal life."

"Oh, yes, it does."

Lines marred his striking features. "Be honest with me, Abby. What are you really saying?"

She couldn't avoid this. "I don't want an affair with you!"

Raoul's black eyes pierced hers like lasers. His hands gripped her shoulders. "That's what you think I want?"

She averted her eyes. "I don't know anymore. I could never be intimate with you and then just fly away as if it never happened. That's why I'd like you to take me back to the apartment now."

"Are you saying this because Nigel is still in your heart and that's what you can't get over?"

"No—" she cried softly. "All feeling for him was burned out of me the second I saw pictures of his children and realized his wife was telling the truth. I honestly haven't thought about him since."

"Even so, being intimate takes time to get over and it hasn't been that long since you broke it off with him."

She eased away from Raoul. "You don't understand. I never went to bed with him. We were going to go away over Christmas to be together for the first time. Thank providence his wife came to the office that day and opened my eyes."

"Are you saying you've never made love?" Raoul sounded incredulous.

"That's right."

"Not even with the other man?"

"I couldn't until I knew my heart. That moment never came." She folded her arms to her waist. "Does that shock you?"

"Yes."

"It wasn't because I was afraid of intimacy. But I didn't think it fair to sleep with him before telling him I couldn't marry him. I did love him, but not enough. However, the same can't be said about you and Angélique."

His black brows knit together. "What are you

talking about? I told you my marriage lacked the passion of a real marriage. We slept together in order to have a baby. But after Nicolette was born, I didn't touch my wife again."

She moaned. "But Jean-Marc said—"

"I can just imagine what my brother said," he cut her off. "But he didn't live with me and Angélique behind closed doors. I'd like you to tell me what Jean-Marc said."

"He said several things, among them that Solange was waiting until your pain lifted."

His head reared. "You and I have already had this conversation. She'll have to wait forever. As for Nicolette, she definitely took a part of my heart with her. And I *was* grief stricken, but it was because I could never love Angélique the way a husband should love his wife. I'll pay a price for that to the end of my days. I'm not an honorable man, Abby."

A bleak expression had broken out on his handsome face, filling her with turmoil.

"Raoul—surely you don't mean that! You *can't* mean it. When you gave in to your mother and father's wishes to marry her, Angélique knew you weren't in love with her. But she married you anyway."

He shook his head. "But it was wrong."

"How can you say that? You gave her a beautiful life, and you had a baby who turned out to be a great blessing. Nicolette brought both of you joy. For you to go on punishing yourself makes no sense. You were forced into that marriage because of a lie. Now you're free to marry the woman you love."

His pain-filled eyes searched hers. "Are you telling me you could marry me, knowing my history at this point?"

"But we're not talking about me."

"Now you're deliberately misunderstanding me." He grasped her upper arms. His black gaze burned with an inner fire she could feel. "I want to marry you, Abby Grant. Tonight if we could. I want it more than anything I've ever wanted in my whole life."

She gasped.

"What else could all this be about?" He shook

her gently. "Losing my family within seconds of the crash has taught me one important lesson. We don't know how much time we have before life strikes a blow. The idea of meeting you and not being able to love you forever is anathema to me. Are you listening to me?"

It was a good thing he was holding on to her, or she would have fainted on the spot. "You couldn't want me for your wife, Raoul. I'm afraid I'd be an embarrassment to you."

"*Embarrassment*—don't you have that turned around? Be honest. In your wildest dreams you couldn't have imagined a man like me coming into your life."

"That's because you had a special destiny decreed generations ago. All that you are, your identity, everything is tied up here in Burgundy."

"But my curse is that I have good and bad baggage. The question is, why would a brilliant American college professor who has lived by the Pacific Ocean all her life want to leave family and country for an entrenched French vintner?"

"Raoul. Listen to me, please. I'm afraid I couldn't measure up to you."

"That argument doesn't hold water and you know it," he bit out. "It's because you're afraid to take a chance on me. Admit it—" His voice throbbed.

"Don't you ever say that!" she cried. "You're the most wonderful man I've ever known. You wouldn't have had to tell me about the poem for me to come with you. Aren't you convinced yet that I'd give anything to lie in your arms and never have to leave? From the beginning, I wasn't able to hide my feelings from you. Only love could have made me drive to France with you in the first place."

"Then will you marry me right away? We'll say our vows at the deputy mayor's office in Dijon. He was a judge and is a good friend of mine with the power to waive the banns requirement." He leaned closer and pressed a kiss to her lips to stifle any other words. "A civil marriage is mandatory before we could be married in church."

Abby couldn't keep up with him. "Stop! You're going too fast. I have to think about it before I can say yes."

She felt his hard body shudder in response. "While you do that, you're in too much danger from me here, so I'm going to take you back to the apartment."

"But where will you be?"

"In my office doing a ton of work that has backed up. When I pick you up in the morning, I'll expect an answer from you."

Before she knew it, he'd driven her back to the *petit château*. After an intense kiss at the entrance to her apartment, he eased away. *"Dors bien, ma belle."*

She watched him drive away in the night. Abby held on to the door handle, shaking because his words had taken hold inside her.

He wanted to marry her. He'd already talked about a date…

With her mind reeling, Abby went inside her apartment and curled up on the bed, throwing a duvet over her.

Raoul's first marriage had been forced on him. It wasn't because of a great love. He'd admitted how painful it had been. But the fact that he felt so undeserving of a woman's love was much more painful to her.

Once again she could imagine what her friends would say. *You can't marry a man this soon. You've been swept away on a riptide.*

But Abby was so desperately in love with him, she couldn't imagine life without him. Yet she'd never felt so conflicted in her life.

Turning to the two people whose advice she treasured most in life, she phoned home. To her relief her mother answered. It had to be late afternoon.

"Abby, darling—I'm so glad you called. We haven't heard from you since your vacation started."

"I know. I'm sorry, but so much has happened, I hardly to know where to begin. Is Dad home yet?"

"No. He has a meeting and will be late."

"Tell him I love him. Mom? I need to talk to you. Is this a good time?"

"What do you think."

"Will you play King Solomon for a few minutes?"

There was a long pause. "That's the most serious question you ever asked me."

"That's because it is." In a shaky voice Abby said, "I've met the great love of my life. He has asked me to marry him right away. There's no way to describe him."

"Try."

For the next half hour Abby poured out her soul to her. When she'd finished talking, she wiped her eyes and waited for her mother to say something. "Mom?"

"King Solomon would tell you to wait and give it time. But I'm your mother and I'm convinced you're too in love to take anyone's advice. You said you have to be married in a civil ceremony first. So why don't you do it without telling anyone?

"I'm sure your father would tell you the same

thing. While you go through the waiting period so you can be married in the church, you'll know if you've made a mistake. Then you can tell the whole world, or not."

Abby let out the breath she'd been holding. "Thank you, Mom. That's what I was praying to hear. It won't be a mistake! I'm sending you some pictures of him and the estate on my phone right now."

Again, Abby waited to hear her mother's response. Finally, she said, "He's the most gorgeous man I ever laid eyes on."

"Mom—"

"I may be your mother, but I'm not blind. Please don't tell your father what I said."

Abby chuckled. "It'll be our secret. Have you scrolled to the picture of the château yet?"

"Oh, my heavens!"

"That's what I said."

"Your father's not going to believe it."

"I'm afraid Dad's not going to approve of doing anything too soon."

"You're right. He won't be happy."

"Maybe you shouldn't say anything to Steve or Nadine yet."

"Don't worry. I'll keep this under wraps until we hear from you again. All we want is your happiness, darling."

"I love you, Mom. More than you know. I promise to call soon."

Abby got ready for bed, but she barely slept waiting for morning to come.

CHAPTER NINE

WHEN MORNING CAME, Raoul texted Abby that he was driving over to the apartment. By the time he arrived in front, his nerves were so shot he was trembling and felt ill. If she told him she couldn't marry him…

Abby opened her door to him, wearing a creamy linen blouse with a wrap-around khaki skirt. He walked her inside and reached for her, kissing her so soundly they were both weaving by the time he allowed her to breathe. "Did you get any sleep?"

She avoided his eyes, terrifying him. "No. I talked to my mother last night. Dad wasn't home. I told her everything."

His insides froze. "Abby?"

"She said if it's going to be a mistake, it would

be better we have a civil ceremony first. Then no one will have to know."

Raoul could hardly breathe. "Is that how you feel? That it will be a mistake?"

"Not if we set some parameters. How do you feel about a working wife?"

With that one question, his taut hard body relaxed. She lifted her green eyes to his, revealing a shine that almost blinded him.

"You realize I'll have to find a teaching position somewhere around here, and I'll have to go to school to learn French."

"Abby—" he whispered her name again, and started to reach for her.

"And one more thing. I want a baby with you so badly I expect to get pregnant ASAP. If that happens, we'll work out everything else."

In the next breath he cupped her face in his hands. "You just gave me the answer I've been dying for. All my adult life I wondered when or if the right woman would come along. When I found you sitting on the train station bench, my heart almost failed me. Somehow I knew my search was over."

"So did I. It was a feeling that grew stronger with every passing minute," she murmured against his lips, hugging the life out of him. "I love you so terribly."

"Je t'aime, mon amour."

Raoul began kissing her with abandon. The freedom to love her had caused him to forget everything else. His hunger had taken over and he couldn't get enough of her. He buried his face in her neck.

"Our wedding day can't come fast enough, but I agree with your mother. I don't want anyone to know we got married until after the fact. By the time my family comes to grips with it, they'll be ready to see us married in the church. But I'm going to have a devil of a time pretending that nothing is going on when all I want to do is steal you away for weeks on end. Come on. We have work to do."

"Where are we going?"

"To my office. I'll have our breakfast brought

in from the château kitchen. While we eat, we'll start to make arrangements. The first thing we have to do is meet with Boris Rochefort, our attorney in Dijon who's licensed to practice law both here and in the States. He'll issue us affidavits of law and marital status. I'll also need a copy of Angélique's death certificate. Next we'll go to Dr. Filbert's office for our medical exams."

"Ooh. I forgot about that. Can you trust these men not to tell anyone about us?"

"If they want to keep their jobs." She laughed. "Before we leave, you need to send for a certified birth certificate."

She leaned over to kiss him again. "I brought one with my passport, just in case of some emergency. Who would have thought I was going to need it to get married to the most marvelous man on earth?"

He gathered her in his arms. "You've made me so happy, I'm never going to let you out of my sight."

"Promise? Oh, Raoul." She wrapped her arms

around his neck, but he was too hungry for her and knew this couldn't go on if they were going to make the appointments he'd set up for them.

After they left her apartment and ate breakfast in his office, they drove to Dijon in the Maserati. Once they'd gone through the motions to receive the various certificates, Raoul took her to the city hall where he introduced Abby to Deputy Mayor Judge Tibault. His friend would marry them and waive the banns. Because of his packed schedule, the soonest their wedding could take place was nine o'clock on Thursday morning, three days away.

By evening they dined at the Coin Caché. He reached across the small round table for her hand. "I brought you here to eat their two specialties: eggs in red wine, and Paris-Brest."

"What is that?"

"One of my favorite desserts. It was named for a bicycle race between those two cities."

She smiled. "Now I understand."

"It's a wheel-shaped pastry, made with a praline-flavored filling."

"Umm. That sounds delicious. When I cook for you, I'm afraid I won't be making anything so exotic."

"You like to cook?"

"I love it when I have the time. I'll fix you some American dishes I know you'll like."

"Abby—" Emotion made his throat swell. Instead of talking, he kissed the palm of her hands before letting it go.

"I'm so excited to become your wife, Raoul. Everything that other wives have been doing since time immemorial, I'll be able to do for you. For the next three days I don't think I'll be able to sleep."

"Don't plan on getting any after we're married."

She answered back with fire in those gorgeous green eyes. "I was going to tell you the same thing."

"Chérie—I know you don't want me spending money on you, but since your family isn't

here, will you at least let me buy you a dress to wear on Thursday?"

"Yes." Her answer surprised and pleased him. "I've seen a few bridal shops while we've been going in and out of buildings. Will you have time tomorrow to drive me there?"

"What do *you* think. Speaking of driving, we need to talk about a car for you."

"I left my old Honda at home in my parents' garage." Abby finished the last of her pastry. "When we get back to my apartment, I'll call my folks when we can talk to dad. I'll add that they can keep the car. They'll want to talk to you."

"I'm looking forward to telling them that they've raised the loveliest woman on both sides of the Atlantic."

"I love you," she whispered.

"I need to take you home where we can be alone. When are you going to tell your friends about us?"

She gave him an impish smile. "After the deed is done."

Raoul burst into laughter, loving this woman beyond anything he thought possible. On the way home he clung to her hand. It was still hard to believe she'd agreed to spend the rest of her life with him. That's what he told her parents when they called them later that night on her phone.

To Raoul's surprise her father was friendly and made him laugh. "I've never been able to afford the Decorvet Pinot Noir. It's too high-end for anyone I know. My daughter has come a long way," he teased, emphasizing the *long*.

Raoul said, "I'll send you a case."

"If you're trying to win my approval, that's the way to do it. But seriously, our daughter has never sounded happier in her life."

"You have our blessing." This from her mother.

"Thank you. Later on, we'd like to have a church wedding where you and your family can come," Raoul interjected. "It will be my pleasure to fly you over and back."

"We'll look forward to that. Be sure to send pictures as soon as you're married in Dijon."

"It'll be the first thing we do, Mom," Abby spoke up. "Give my love to everyone."

When they hung up, he wrapped her in his arms. "They're incredibly nice for two parents who couldn't possibly think this will work. The first thing I'm going to do tomorrow is send a shipment of wine to them."

"They'll love it. *I* love it. They're already so impressed with you, and I'm so madly in love with you it's pathetic, even if your phone is ringing."

Raoul pulled it out of his pocket. "It's my father."

"Go ahead and get it."

He kissed her thoroughly. "This is for business. I'll call you in the morning and we'll make our plans."

She walked him to the door. "I'll be counting the hours."

After he walked out to the car, Abby shut the door. There couldn't be a happier woman in all France tonight. She hurried into the bedroom and got ready for bed. Knowing she wouldn't be able to go to sleep yet, she reached for her laptop as she got under the sheets.

The first thing she did was write a lengthy letter to the head of the literature department at San José State to let them know she was getting married and wouldn't be returning in the fall. She would hand write an official letter of resignation later, but they needed to know her plans immediately.

Before she'd met Raoul, she couldn't have imagined this scenario, not when she'd worked so long and hard for that position. But the world had changed on its axis when Raoul had come into her life. To think it hadn't even been a whole week!

With her missive sent, she got busy on another project. It had been a long time since she'd gone shopping for clothes, let alone a wedding dress. For the next hour she looked at everything under the sun. By the time she was ready to shut her computer off, she knew exactly the style and color she wanted. She'd pick up some other items too, including a few nightgowns.

Abby got out of bed long enough to put the laptop back on the table and turn off the overhead light. Only a few more days and she'd be going to bed with Raoul every night. She climbed under the covers, imagining he was with her.

The next morning she got up to shower and wash her hair. Since she would be picking out her wedding outfit, she wore her sundress with the jacket to look a little more dressed up. More new clothes were needed, but she'd worry about that later.

Her phone didn't ring until eight-thirty. She hoped everything was all right and picked up after the first ring. "Raoul?"

"Forgive me for not calling sooner. I'm afraid our plans are going to have to change today." Disappointment swamped her. "I'll explain later, but I'm going to be tied up with business until the afternoon, so I've instructed a maid from the château kitchen to bring you breakfast.

224 CAPTIVATED BY THE BROODING BILLIONAIRE

"She should be there any minute. Anything else you want to eat, you'll find in your kitchen. Feel free to explore the property or do whatever you want. I can't give you a definite time when I'll be back, but I promise to call and keep you informed." He sounded rushed.

"You always do. Is everything okay?"

"It will be when I put out this latest fire."

This was his life and she'd better get used to it. "Good luck, my love."

No sooner had she hung up than the maid knocked on the door. Abby thanked her and walked into the sitting room with the delicious-looking meal. Once she'd eaten her fill, she walked back to her computer while she waited for Raoul.

At noon he returned to the apartment. He swept her in his arms. "What have you been doing?"

"Last night I sent in my resignation to the department. While I was waiting for you to come just now, I received an answer from Dr. Thurman. I'll show it to you later."

He walked her out to the car and they took off. "Did he say he'd make you a full *professeur* to keep you on?"

She smiled. "It wouldn't have mattered if he'd offered me the moon. You have no idea how much I love you." After kissing him again she said, "I wrote to Magda. If she hadn't chosen me to help on that script, I would never have ended up in Switzerland and met you. To think if the girls and I had arrived a day later…"

"I don't want to think about it, Abby. It was meant to be. Do you know what kind of a dress you want to buy for our wedding?"

"Yes! I saw exactly what I wanted online last night. If you'll drive us to the Grace Loves Lace shop, that should be the only place we have to go. I hope you won't mind staying in the car. I don't want you to see it until Thursday."

He found it on the address locater. "After it's put in a bag, I'll come in long enough to pay for it."

"I'll need some shoes too, and some lingerie.

I can get everything there at the same time. I promise I won't take a long time."

One thing he knew about Abby. She wasn't one to play games and always kept her promises. After he dropped her off in front, he parked and made arrangements for their honeymoon. He had a surprise for her.

Before long she waved to him from the entrance. He went inside to pay the clerk. After helping her out to the car with her garment bag and packages, he took her to dinner at a sidewalk café.

"You look happy." In truth she was radiant.

"I am, but I'm wondering how I'm going to make it through to Thursday. I wish we were married right now."

He'd been thinking that for days now and took her back to the car. Before starting the engine, Raoul took a deep breath. "I have a lot of work to do, which will help me stay away from you tomorrow. As for tonight, it's getting late. I'm going to take you back to the apartment and we won't be seeing each other again until Thursday morning."

She chuckled. "I didn't know you were so old-fashioned about not seeing the bride before the wedding."

"Surely you realize I have to let you go right now because I don't trust myself to be around you any longer. At 6:30 a.m. Thursday, my assistant, Félix, will come for you in his car."

"I don't understand."

"Gossip will follow that you're moving out of the apartment for good. Which you are. He'll load your luggage and everything you've bought. Be sure to wear something to suggest you're dressed to travel. He'll drive you to the helipad beyond the château and my pilot will fly you to a hotel in Dijon where I'll be waiting."

"So this is it?" The disappointment in her eyes made him want to drive into the night with her and never return.

"It would be a mistake to touch you again once we get back to the estate. Just remember that the next time we do this, you'll be my wife." On that fierce note he leaned toward her and kissed her fully, losing himself in the love this magnificent woman miraculously returned.

Raoul saw Abby to the door of her apartment with her things, but he didn't reach for her. She trembled uncontrollably when she heard him drive away.

Everything had to be kept secret. It seemed wrong, but her mother thought it was best and she had to trust Raoul that this was the only way for them. As soon as they were married, they'd go immediately to the château and announce it to his family in his grandparents' suite.

Trying to throw off her worry, she took out her dress and opened the other bags. She wished her friends were here to see the knee-length white lace dress and celebrate with her.

Abby hadn't planned to tell them until after the wedding, but she was too excited to hold back. Since it was late, she texted both of them and to let them know what was going on before she went to bed.

When morning came she still hadn't heard back from them. Afraid that Raoul might send a maid with her breakfast, she repacked everything and put it out of sight. Since she couldn't stand to be alone with her thoughts any longer, she looked up some addresses in Dijon, then phoned for a taxi.

After it arrived, she asked the driver to take her to the jewelry store address on her list. It was very small and they spoke English. For the next hour she looked at all the men's wedding bands. "Do you have any special, unique kinds of bands?"

The jeweler brought out another tray. When she saw the yellow gold one with a small cluster of round purple jewels in the center, she knew she'd found what she wanted. "This looks like it was made for a vintner."

"Indeed it was." The jeweler looked pleased. "I've been wondering when someone would buy it."

She smiled. "I think it's been waiting for me. What's the price?"

When he told her, she blinked. It would take all the money she'd planned to spend on her vacation, but she decided it didn't matter because she only intended to be married once. She could never do enough for Raoul to show him how much she loved him.

"Will you engrave something for me on the inside?"

"Bien sûr." He handed her a pad and pencil.

Abby printed the words for *my beloved* in French and the date of the wedding.

Mon bien-aimé, le 9 juin.

"It won't be ready for a couple of hours."

"Then I'll be back." She paid him with her credit card and left to get lunch at a café she'd seen around the corner on her way here. Once she'd given her order, her phone rang. Her pulse raced, thinking it was Raoul. But when she pulled it out of her purse, she saw the caller ID and answered.

"Zoe?"

"So you're really going to do it!" she blurted first thing.

"Yes."

"Without giving me or Ginger a chance to be there?"

"We'll get married again in church in front of all our family and friends, but we have to be married civilly first." She gripped the phone tighter. "Do you think I'm crazy?"

"Yes, but I can tell you're so in love with him you can't help yourself. Just remember that Ginger and I will be thinking of you tomorrow, even though you won't be thinking about us. Now I've got to run to catch the ferry. God bless. May you have joy, Abby."

Joy was the right word.

Abby ate her pasta salad and then did some window shopping until it was time to pick up the ring. When she walked into the shop, he had it waiting for her.

"Do you want this gift wrapped?"

"No." She inspected the inscription. "This is perfect. Thank you. Just put it in the little box."

"Très bien."

With it tucked safely in her purse, she started to leave, then went back to the counter. "Do you have any pins for a woman to wear on a suit jacket or dress? Maybe something with flowers?"

He frowned. "What do you mean exactly?"

"Well, I'm getting married in the morning to an important vintner in the region, and I'd like to have a gift to give my fiancé's mother. Nothing extravagant, but something meaningful that says I love her wonderful son."

"Let me think. I'll have to go in back where I keep my special collections." He came out a minute later and laid a little one-inch gold pin on the velvet. It was a vine with enamel purple grapes and one enameled white flower at the top.

Abby shook her head. "I can't believe you have something like this."

"Burgundy is famous for its vineyards."

"It's exactly what I was hoping to find. How much is it?"

"Consider it a wedding present from my shop. I hope you'll come in again."

"Of course I will! I can't thank you enough. Will you please gift wrap it for me?"

She was so thrilled with her purchases, she couldn't stand still. As soon as he handed it to her, she put it in her purse and hurried outside to a *tête de taxi*. When she said the Decorvet Domaine, the driver nodded and they took off for Vosne-Romanée.

En route she received a text from Ginger.

I was right. He did get to your romantic soul. Forget everything I ever said. I couldn't be happier for you.

Tears stung Abby's eyes to have her friends' blessings.

When the driver reached the gate, he made a phone call and the doors swung open to let them through. She gave him directions to the *petit château* and paid him before getting out of the taxi.

For the rest of the day she did work on the internet. First she looked up the University of Burgundy located in Dijon and discovered that the humanities and sciences were well represented on the main campus with law, medicine and literature in separate buildings. She didn't know if she could ever get a teaching position there, but it wouldn't hurt to inquire.

Then she looked up where to get French lessons. Abby could go many directions, but thought it might work to hire a private tutor. She found the names of three qualified instructors and phoned them for more information.

After saying she would get back to them, she fixed herself some food from the kitchen and then sat down to watch TV. But she could hardly concentrate while waiting for Raoul to get in touch with her. She knew he wouldn't be coming over, but when it got to be nine o'clock, it surprised her that there'd been no phone call.

It wasn't until she climbed in bed and set her alarm for six a.m. that she received the long-awaited text.

Tomorrow every dream of mine is going to come true.

She sent a text back.

Get a good sleep, beloved. You're going to be loved the way no one has ever been loved before.

After putting the phone on the side table, she buried her face in the pillow, whispering his name.

Raoul waited near the landing pad at the Dijon-Bourgogne Airport in the Maserati. He rechecked his watch. Five after seven. The helicopter should be here by now. *Mon Dieu...* if anything unforeseen happened to her at this point, he wouldn't want to go on living.

He was ready to contact his pilot when he saw the helicopter approach. The second it set down, he got out of the car and hurried toward the door even though the rotors were still going. His pilot opened it and there stood Abby who

236 CAPTIVATED BY THE BROODING BILLIONAIRE

cried out his name and climbed right out into his arms.

"*Dieu merci* you're here." He covered her face with kisses. "Another minute and I would have lost my mind."

"You're not the only one." She kissed him with enough passion to rock him back on his heels.

"Let's get you in the car with all your things and I'll drive us to the hotel near the city hall where you can change."

With the help of his trusted pilot, they stowed all of her things. Raoul waved him off and got in behind the wheel. He shot her a piercing glance. "Are you ready?"

She reached for his hand and squeezed her answer hard.

Once they reached the hotel parking, they took only the things she'd need for the ceremony and hurried inside. Everything else would stay locked in the car.

He'd gotten them a room on the second floor near the elevator where they'd both change.

Raoul had ordered breakfast. They ate quickly. As soon as she disappeared into the bathroom with her garment bag, he put on his white dress shirt and formal gray suit.

Then he waited with pounding heart for her to emerge. When she walked out a few minutes later, he couldn't catch his breath. Her dress, made of the finest white Chantilly lace, covered her from her neck to her wrists, and followed her curving shape to her knees. On her feet were matching lace high heels.

"Abby—" His voice shook.

He took one white rose from the white rose bouquet he'd had made up for her and tucked it behind her ear.

Abby's green eyes roved over him hungrily, feeding his desire. "I'm the luckiest woman in the whole world."

Raoul handed her the bouquet of roses and her purse. "Let's go get married."

A taxi waited for them out in front of the hotel and drove them to the entrance of the city hall. As he helped her out to the pavement, a volley of whistles sounded. She literally stopped traffic as they walked up the steps into the building.

He cupped her elbow and walked to the room where Deputy Mayor Judge Tibault was waiting for them. The older man couldn't take his eyes off Abby. After introducing them to the two witnesses who'd been brought in from the other room, he winked at her. "No wonder Raoul wanted the banns waived. If I were thirty years younger…"

Abby blushed and clung to Raoul.

"If you're ready, then stand in front of my desk and hold hands."

She put her bouquet on a chair, then placed her right hand in his.

"Abby Cederlof Grant and Raoul Capet Regnac Decorvet, do you both come together of your own free will in the prefecture of Dijon on this ninth day of June to be united in marriage?"

"Yes," they said in unison.

"Raoul? Do you take Abby to be your wife?"

"I do"

"Do you promise to love, honor, cherish and

protect her, through the good and the bad, forsaking all others and holding only unto her?"

"I do"

"Abby? Do you take Raoul to be your husband?"

"I do," sounded her tremulous voice.

"Do you promise to love, honor, cherish and protect him, through the good and the bad, forsaking all others and holding only unto him?"

"Yes," she said emotionally.

"Abby? Hold out your left hand. Raoul? Repeat after me. Abby Grant, I take thee to be my wife, to have and to hold, in sickness and in health, for richer or for poorer, and I promise my love to you. With this ring I thee wed."

After saying the words, Raoul pulled the diamond ring from his pocket and slid it on to her ring finger. Her eyes took in the three-carat diamond solitaire before she lifted moist eyes to him. They burned with love.

"Abby? Do you have a ring for him?"

"Yes."

Her answer came as a complete surprise.

"Raoul? Extend your left hand."

He did his bidding.

"Abby? Repeat after me. I take Raoul Decorvet to be my husband, to have and to hold, in sickness and in health, for richer or for poorer, and I promise my love to you. With this ring I thee wed."

He looked down as she put it on his ring finger. A gasp escaped his lips. The design of the purple gem stones resembling a cluster of pinot noir grapes set in gold shook him to the very core of his body. Was this what she'd been doing when he'd found out she'd left the estate yesterday in a taxi?

"Just as two very different threads woven in opposite directions can form a beautiful tapestry, so can your two lives merge together to form a very beautiful marriage. To make it work will take love.

"Love should be the core. Love is the reason you are here. But it also will take trust—to know in your hearts you want the best for each other. It will take dedication—to stay open to one another; to learn and to grow together even when this is not always so easy to do.

"It will take faith to be willing to go forward to tomorrow, never really knowing what tomorrow will bring. In addition, it will take commitment to hold true to the journey you both now pledge to share together.

"In so much as the two of you have agreed to live together in matrimony and have promised your love for each other by these vows, I now declare you to be husband and wife. Congratulations. You may kiss your bride."

"Darling," she cried as he covered her mouth with his own. All the love he could ever hope for or imagine was surrendered to him in a kiss that went on forever.

He rocked her body in his arms, never wanting to let her go. But when he opened his eyes, he realized that the deputy mayor, who had a broad smile on his face, was waiting for them to join the world once more.

Raoul looked down at her. "Madame Decorvet. Do you have any idea what it means to call you Madame Decorvet? I think we need to get a room of our own."

"Just as soon as you both sign the marriage certificate."

His bride blushed again before they wrote their signatures. Raoul asked Tibault to take some pictures of them with his phone. With that done, they shook the older man's hand, then Raoul swept his bride out of the room and the building to their same taxi. The driver knew ahead of time where to take them.

Once in the backseat, Raoul pulled her onto his lap, ignoring the flowers and kissed her passionately until they arrived at the hotel. When they got out and reached their room, he carried her over the threshold and followed her down onto the bed.

"I can't begin to express all the feelings exploding inside me, Abby. All I know is, I adore you, *mon épouse*. It's killing me that we have to drive back to the château right now. Once we make our announcement to the family, then we'll drive to the cottage and forget the world."

She caressed the side of his jaw with her hand. "I know how important this is, especially for your grandparents' sake. They love you so much and are waiting. And I haven't forgotten we were seen by officials who will tell the press. The news of our marriage will be all over French TV by tonight. We *have* to tell your family immediately.

"I did some research about you. You're one of the most important men in France." Her eyes misted over again. "It's an honor to be your wife. I'm still having a hard time believing that this is really happening."

"You're going to know it all right, once I get you home and in my arms. I may never let you go. This ring I'm wearing… No man was ever given a greater treasure."

"There's an inscription."

Excited, he removed it and read it aloud.

After giving her another deep kiss, he rolled away and got to his feet. "The sooner we leave, the sooner our new life will begin."

Still wearing their wedding clothes, they gathered up their few things and took everything to the car. As they left the city and headed for home, he reached for her hand. "For the first time in my life, I'm seeing my world in Technicolor. It's all because of you."

CHAPTER TEN

"THAT'S EXACTLY HOW it feels," Abby exclaimed. "While you're driving, I'm going to phone my parents. Can I use yours? I'll send the photos at the same time."

Raoul handed it to her.

"First I'm going to take a picture of this gorgeous diamond ring you gave me. I love a solitaire more than anything. How did you know?"

"It has a pureness and reminds me of you."

Everything he said touched her heart.

By the time she got off the phone, they'd reached the estate and Raoul drove them to the south entrance of the château. Suddenly the gravity of their announcement and what it would mean to his family took hold of her. When he turned off the engine and helped her out of the car, she hugged him hard.

"Don't be afraid. We'll just have to give them time. Remember part of our vows? It will take faith to be willing to go forward to tomorrow, never really knowing what tomorrow will bring."

"I know." She pressed a kiss to his lips. "I have faith in you."

He checked his watch. "We have ten minutes before everyone will congregate. Let's go greet my grandparents first."

With his arm around her waist, he ushered her inside and up the stairs to the second floor. After a knock, he opened the double doors. Lisette had wheeled his grandparents into the main salon. She congratulated them first.

"Ah—" his grandmother cried when she saw them. "That lace is breathtaking. How beautiful you look, Abby!"

"Thank you. It's because I'm so happy to be married to your grandson. Doesn't he look handsome in his gray suit?"

His grandfather smiled and nodded.

"Papi? Mamie? May I present my wife, the

joy of my life. Look what she gave me." He walked over to the old man so he could examine the ring.

Abby hurried to his grandmother and gave her a kiss on both cheeks. They both marveled over the dazzling diamond.

She grasped Abby's hand. "I've never seen him this happy."

"That's what my parents said about me when we sent pictures to them a little while ago. We're going to have a wedding picture made up for you."

"We would love it. Abby—don't let what anyone says or does disturb you," she whispered.

"I won't," she whispered back. "We know you and your husband approve of our marriage. That means the world to us."

"This is a difficult family."

"I think all families are, a little."

She stared at Abby. "I can see you are the right one for him."

"I'm glad if you think so."

"I'll pray for you."

Her words stayed with Abby as they heard voices in the entry. Raoul reached her side and put his arm around her shoulders. Soon the family entered the salon. She counted at least twenty-five members. She recognized Jean-Marc, Gilles, Paul and Raoul's father, who sat in his wheelchair, but not anyone else.

The shock on each face told a story Abby would never forget. Raoul's arm tightened. "Thank you all for dropping everything to come here today. I wanted you to know that Abby Grant, the light of my life, became my wife this morning at the *mairie* in Dijon by Deputy Mayor Tibault. We'll be married at the church in Dijon in a few weeks."

Before he could say another word, she heard a cry and the pregnant brunette woman standing next to Paul left the suite. That had to be Josette.

Her husband walked over to Abby and Raoul. "Welcome to the family." He kissed her on both cheeks. After giving Raoul a hug, he hurried after his wife.

In the next breath Raoul's father, with a scowl

on his face, barked to Jean-Marc to wheel him out of the room. The lovely older woman who'd been standing next to him—the thin one with the reddish-blond hair who had to be Raoul's mother—seemed to pale. She looked conflicted before following her husband out of the salon.

"Just a minute, darling," Abby said to Raoul. Then she ran after his mother and caught up with her in the entry hall. "I wanted to give you this." She put the tiny wrapped gift in her hand. "I love Raoul desperately and want us to be friends."

His mother looked utterly bewildered before Abby ran back to Raoul, passing his two aunts and their families who were walking out.

It was like watching dominos fall one by one.

"Congratulations," said one of the men who resembled Raoul's father. "I hope you'll be happy."

"Thank you, Oncle Pierre."

The other older man who stood next to Pierre nodded to Raoul. "I must say I'm surprised you didn't pick a woman of our own nationality, but I wish you both well."

"*Merci, Oncle Lucien.* That means a lot. To be honest, love picked me," he said, kissing Abby's cheek.

Gilles frowned at Raoul. He said something in French Abby didn't understand and strode out of the salon behind his father.

Abby felt like she'd been watching a bizarre play, not believing that anyone could sketch characters as unbelievable as these real people. Did inheriting a title truly do this kind of damage?

When his aunt left the room, Raoul pulled Abby into his arms and held her for a long time. She wanted to tell him they should leave here and never come back. No one deserved this kind of treatment.

There were so many things she wanted to say to him, but she knew she couldn't. This was his life. He'd been totally honest about it. She'd just pledged to love and support him.

Learn and grow together even when this is not always so easy to do.

Those words were part of the vows she'd taken just hours ago. She *had* to honor them, but she knew it was going to be the hardest test she would ever have to pass in this life.

The sadness in his grandparents' eyes since the rest of the family had come into the salon haunted her. Raoul had clung to them all these years for a reason. Well now he had Abby too! She would be his rock.

When Raoul let her go, she walked over to his grandfather and gave him a hug. "Now that we'll be living in the cottage, we'll come to visit you every day. Raoul needs your help and your wisdom," she murmured near his ear.

She felt him reach for her hand and squeeze it hard, but she knew he was getting tired. So was his grandmother.

Raoul blew both of them a kiss, then grasped her hand and they left the suite for the car. Neither of them spoke as he started the engine and drove to the cottage. When they arrived, he sat there without moving. "I knew it would be bad, but I can see I should never have subjected you to this."

"But you're too honorable to behave in any other way."

"Why did you run after my mother?"

"To give her a little gift for having the most fabulous son on earth."

"Abby—"

"Tell me something. Why did your sister walk out like that? What's the real reason?"

"Father should have made her the head of the *domaine*. She's as capable of managing it as I am. When Angélique and the baby died, she didn't think I'd get married again. With no child to come after me, it would mean their son, Maurice, would be the next one in line. Seeing me married again, she's afraid we'll have a baby and that will be the end of any hope she has. Paul's promotion still won't bring her what she'd hoped for."

"But she's your sister."

"And we love each other. We've shared good

times too, but you have to understand that my father's decision to name me has hurt her and my aunts who are equally capable of running the estate. He sees running the grape business as men's work."

Raoul turned a solemn face to her. "This is nothing against you personally, Abby. My mother would have stayed to welcome you if my father hadn't forced Jean-Marc to wheel him out. She's never had the courage to stand up to him when something important mattered to her."

"We're all too human at times. What did Gilles say to you? Did he hurt you?"

"No. He said I was a damn lucky man."

After a dark sound escaped his lips, he helped her from the car. To her surprise he carried her over the threshold. Once inside, they clung to each other.

"Darling? Please don't suffer for my sake. We're home in our happy refuge. This is our *Saint des Saints.* Nothing can touch us here. We have each other. What else do we need? Are you listening to me? You're my everything, Raoul. I ache to love you. Let me show you what you mean to me."

"Abby—" He kissed her mouth. She tasted the salt from his tears. "This was no way to start out our marriage."

"Your grandmother said she'd pray for us."

A sad chuckle escaped. "That sounds like Mamie."

"Guess what? You and I promised to love and cherish each other through the good and the bad. Since we've gotten the bad out of the way really fast, how about you help me out of this dress *toot sweet*?" It was the word for fast in French.

The reaction she'd hoped for came out of Raoul who let out a deep belly laugh. "I think you meant *tout de suite.*"

"Yes. I love the sound of it."

"I love you, *ma femme.* I love every particle of you." He carried her into the bedroom and put her down gently before unfastening the button at the back of her neck. "Get ready to be loved," he warned her.

"I was ready when you brought me to the cottage for the first time, remember?" She undid his tie. "If you want to know a secret, I've been waiting for the *dénouement* since the moment you got out of that old black car how many eons ago?"

He grinned and flung his suit jacket on the chair. "Something tells me my new bride has been studying her French."

"It's a beautiful language." She started unbuttoning his shirt. "Almost as beautiful as you."

"You think a man is beautiful?"

"Not until I met you."

Raoul helped her off with her dress and put the divine white lace concoction on top of his jacket. His eyes burned like black fire as he drew her onto the bed and a husband's desire took over, making her thankful she'd been born a woman.

Three days and nights of nonstop loving had made a new man out of Raoul. They'd wanted for nothing. Before the wedding, he'd had the cottage stocked with everything they'd need so nothing could disturb them. Their world was so perfect he refused to let anything or one intrude on their happiness.

Abby was not only his wife, she was his generous lover who poured out her heart and soul to him while they worshipped each other with their bodies. Hers was glorious. He loved her with a passion that scared him whenever he thought of losing her.

Monday morning he awakened early with a desire so intense for her, he rolled her closer while she was still asleep and started kissing her. Her lovely legs twined with his. She made little sounds until her eyes opened. Her seductive smile set him on fire.

She rubbed his jaw, which needed a shave. "I thought I wore you out in the middle of the night. What are you doing awake again?"

"As if you didn't know, *mon amour.*"

Her voice caught. "Do you think all newly-weds feel the way we do?"

"Only if they're in love the way we are, which

is rare. I've been lying here trying not to think how I would ever handle losing you."

"Raoul—" She leaned over him with a little frown. "What a thing to be thinking!"

"I can't help it. Don't you know you're my heart?"

"If I got started on how much I love you, I'd never stop." She kissed him with a hunger that sent a thrill though him. Two hours later they surfaced long enough for her to escape his arms and get out of bed.

He reached out to trap her hand. "Where do you think you're going?" he asked in a gravelly voice. "I didn't give you permission."

"To shower and fix your breakfast."

"I'd rather you stayed right here. I want to discuss something with you."

"Well, in that case." Abby crawled back in next to him. "Is it serious?"

He kissed her hungrily. "I want to take you on a honeymoon."

"Raoul—that's what I felt we were on when you brought me to Burgundy."

He smoothed the hair from her brow. "I mean a real one."

"Do you have a spot in mind? I read some statistics that showed most French people preferred to vacation in France."

"It's true a lot of them like to camp. But I'd love to spend time on a beach with you."

"Then let's do it when you can get away. I know this isn't the best time."

"How do you know that?"

"I heard you tell Paul you were taking him to Paris sometime this week."

"So I did."

"How long would you be gone?"

"I'll leave in the morning and be away until the next night, but I don't want to leave you. Marrying you has put everything else out of my head."

"While you're gone, I'll start my French lessons. I already have several tutors lined up. When you return, we'll plan a trip after you've looked at your schedule. Living in this cottage with you is the only honeymoon I could ever want."

"I'm thinking the Cinque Terre on the Italian Riviera. You'll be enraptured with the landscape."

"I don't know of it."

"That makes it even better." He kissed her throat. "I want to shower with you and then I'll help you fix breakfast."

She flashed him that come-hither look. He didn't know if she did it on purpose, but it didn't matter because it worked.

"You know I'm learning to like what you eat in the morning? Bread dunked in coffee. It's so easy and nonfattening. It won't do for your wife to put on weight. All I need to hear someone say is 'There goes that plump *Americaine*, waddling her way through the Decorvet vineyard.'"

Raoul burst into laughter. It reverberated throughout the cottage. He'd give her the moon if he could. "After we eat, let's drive into Dijon and buy you a car. You can always use one of mine, but I'm sure you'd like your own. What kind would suit you?"

"Something that's economical and will always start."

He chuckled. "That can be arranged. You're too easy to please."

She slid her arms around his neck beneath the spray of water. "If you don't know it by now, all I want is you." The new ways she showed him proof of her love told him without words this marriage would last forever.

Once they'd dressed and eaten, Raoul left the cottage a new man as they walked out to the Maserati. With his delectable wife clinging to him, the sunny day added a punctuation mark to his mood of euphoria.

By dinnertime she'd decided on a Peugeot 308 in dark blue, but it wouldn't be ready until he returned from Paris.

"Tonight I'd like to take you dancing." He drove them to a popular restaurant/discotheque, but after a few dances he wanted to take her home. "I need to be alone with you as much as possible before I have to leave in the morning."

"I'm so glad you said that," she whispered against his neck.

They couldn't get back to the cottage fast enough. When his alarm went off at six the next morning, they both groaned. Loving her half the night had only made him hungrier for more.

He leaned over her. "I have to meet Paul at the helipad in twenty minutes. Take care and don't let anything happen to you while I'm gone."

"Call me. I won't be able to breathe again until you're back safely."

Abby slept in late. After getting up, she ate some fruit and bread, then started cleaning. Raoul would have sent a maid, but she wanted to keep house for him. She put in a wash and by midafternoon she'd showered and dressed in jeans and a blouse.

He'd given her keys to both cars. She could take either one if she wanted to go out. While she was debating whether to take a drive around the region to get more acquainted with it, she heard a knock on the door. Maybe he'd sent one of the maids after all.

When she opened the door, she received the shock of her life. Josette and their mother stood on the porch. They'd known Raoul had left for Paris with Paul and that she was alone.

"Will you forgive us for coming without phoning you first?" This from his mother who spoke excellent English. "I was afraid you might hang up, and you would have had every right. We haven't even been formally introduced yet. I'm Hélène-Claire. This is my daughter, Josette."

Abby never dreamed she'd see them on the doorstep, not after what happened last Thursday in the grandparents' salon. Even more astounding was that she was wearing the pin Abby had given her. She wore it on the lapel of her pale blue cotton suit. It had to be some kind of a miracle.

"Please come in." She was thankful she'd done the housework. If they'd come a couple of hours sooner and seen the mess… Wait till she told Raoul. "Sit down, won't you?"

"If we're disturbing you, we won't stay."

"But you're not," Abby assured them. "Can I get you coffee or tea?"

Both of them shook their heads. "Nothing thank you."

Josette looked pale and nervous. "The way I treated you and my brother on your wedding day was so inexcusable I know neither of you will ever be able to forgive me. But I had to come and tell you how sorry I am."

"It's all right, Josette. I know our marriage came as a huge shock to everyone. Most of all to me!" The two of them looked surprised. "Raoul and I met under the most unusual circumstances. He was very honest with me about the loss of his wife and baby. I could tell how he'd suffered."

Their eyes filled with tears.

Thrilled that they were listening, Abby broke down and explained everything to them. "My friends were worried about my coming to France with him, but I couldn't not come b-because I'd fallen in love with him that fast," her voice faltered, "and he with me.

"I've cared deeply for two men in my life before Raoul, but I could never see myself married to them. But then I met Raoul and realized he was the one I'd been waiting for. We've come from opposite ends of the world, opposite lifestyles, but we love each other."

"I could tell that," Hélène-Claire murmured. "I saw the way the two of you looked at each other. For the first time in his life, my son looked completely happy and my mother-in-law agrees with me. His marriage to Angélique—"

"I know about that," Abby interrupted. "Nothing else needs to be said. But I know he'll never get over losing his little girl."

"You're very sweet. Raoul couldn't help but fall in love with you." She touched the pin. "This gift you gave me was unexpected for many reasons. It touched my heart."

"I wanted you to have something meaningful. You raised a son who has made me so happy I can't begin to describe how I feel about him. I plan to be the best wife I can be, but I'm going to need help from all of you. My parents are behind our marriage a hundred percent, but what do I, an American literature teacher, know about the family Raoul was born into?"

"I'll help you."

"Thank you, Josette. Raoul loves you and your boy very much. When I met Paul the other day, he let me know how excited he is about the baby that's coming. He was so nice to me."

"Much nicer than I was," she murmured. "He told me my brother deserved a woman like you. Now that we've talked, I couldn't agree with him more."

"Thank you."

"Will you let us make it up to you for the way we treated you?"

"You don't have to do anything. All Raoul would love is to hear what you've just told me."

"We intend to do that," his mother asserted. "What I'd like to do is host a party to welcome you into the family. My husband—"

"Raoul has explained many things to me," she broke in once again. "He suffers a lot of pain."

"Yes, but he needs to demonstrate his love for Raoul, which of course he has always felt. I'm ashamed for his actions as well as the way my two sisters-in-law walked out of the salon. Here's what I'd like to do. Raoul and Paul will be back Wednesday evening. We'll have a family dinner in our suite on the *terrasse*."

Abby got excited. "Let's make it a surprise. Can Maurice come? I want to meet my new nephew."

Josette broke into a genuine smile. "He'd love to be a part of things because he adores my brother."

"Who doesn't?" Abby quipped. "Will the grandparents be able to come?"

"If it's too much for them, we'll visit them after we've eaten dinner."

"And Jean-Marc?"

Josette's brows lifted. "If he can get over his jealousy."

"What do you mean?"

"Our cousin Gilles and my younger brother have a crush on you at the moment."

"Tell Jean-Marc that I found him very charming. If I hadn't met Raoul first..."

At that comment both women laughed. Josette nodded. "I *will* tell him."

Hélène-Claire rose to her feet. "We've kept you long enough. We'll set a time when we know Raoul and Paul will be back from Paris."

"Wonderful!" Nothing sounded more perfect to Abby, who was overjoyed that the two women in Raoul's life had come around to make peace at last. "Let's exchange phone numbers to stay in touch."

When they'd done that, she walked them out to the porch. As soon as they'd driven away, she went inside and checked out some Dijon toy stores. When she found a couple of addresses on the internet, she grabbed her purse and drove the Jaguar into town. What a fantastic car, once she got the hang of it!

Within an hour, she'd purchased a darling musical box called Les Papoum, and a kaleidoscope with a circus motif. You twisted both ends to make different colors. Those gifts would be fun for Maurice.

Raoul phoned just before she went to bed. "I miss you so much I've been no good to Paul today."

"I don't believe it."

"Tell me about your day."

If he only knew. "I slept in, cleaned and drove around in the Jaguar. I promise it's still in one piece, but you'll have to adjust the seat."

His laughter sounded over the line. "I'm going to work all night so we can get home earlier tomorrow."

"What do you want to do when you get here?" she teased. Inside she was struggling to hang on to her secret.

"If you have to ask me that question, then I've been doing something wrong."

Had she said something that worried him? "Darling, I was just checking to make sure you're not tired of me yet."

"Do you honestly think that could ever happen?"

He *was* upset.

"Next time you fly anywhere, I'll go with you, but I can't promise to behave and you'll wish you'd left me behind."

She'd hoped to wring a chuckle from him at least. No such luck.

"I'm never leaving you again." His voice sounded savage. "I'll phone you in the morning. Miss me, *mon amour.*"

"Raoul?"

But he'd hung up. What on earth was wrong?

Their conversation had left her restless and she didn't sleep well. At eight the next morning he phoned her again. She picked up immediately. *"Bonjour, mon mari."* She'd been practicing how to say *my husband.*

"Have you started your tutoring lessons already? Is that where you went in the car yesterday?"

What? "Actually I went shopping."

"I see."

She frowned. "I've been waiting for your call."

"We'll be back at three."

"I'll drive to the helipad and wait for you."

"You don't have to do that."

"What if I want to? I love you."

"I love you too."

Again he hung up, leaving her worried and dissatisfied. Abby flung herself out of bed. Thank heaven he'd be home soon so she could find out what was going on with him.

For the next few hours she sent emails to relatives and friends in and out of the department letting them know that she'd gotten married and where she could be reached. She received a heartfelt congratulations from Magda.

Josette called her later and asked if she wanted to go shopping with her in Dijon while Maurice was napping. Abby had jumped at the chance to get acquainted with Raoul's sister, who bought a becoming aqua maternity dress for the party.

Abby found a green-beaded ruched knee-length sheath dress. Josette assured her Raoul's eyes would pop out when he saw her in it. The dinner was scheduled for six o'clock.

After their return, she put the dress in the closet and drove the Jaguar to the helipad, wearing her jeans and blouse. Raoul had said three, but it was three-fifteen when she heard the sound of the rotors. Soon the helicopter came into view. Her heart thudded as she watched it set down. Out came Paul with a suitcase. Raoul followed with his.

She left the car and ran to hug him. If something was still bothering him, he didn't let it show as he crushed her against him and swung her around. The intensity of his kiss melted her insides before he swept her toward the car. He helped her in the passenger seat and got in the driver's seat out of habit. Paul sat in back.

Abby turned to her brother-in-law. "Did business go well?"

"I never realized how much I didn't know."

"He's going to do great work for us," Raoul commented. He dropped him off at the château, then drove them to the cottage. Her husband was still in an odd mood.

"Before we go inside, I want to know what's wrong. You haven't been yourself since we talked on the phone last night."

He shut off the engine and turned toward her. "The truth?"

"Always."

"I should never have left you this soon after our wedding. When you told me you'd taken a drive and had gone shopping, I knew you couldn't bear to be here alone. You seemed a little evasive. I was angry with myself and I'm afraid I let it show."

"All is forgiven." She might have known that he'd sensed she'd been keeping something from him. Raoul wasn't a man you could toy with, not when it came to his deepest emotions. "I *was* being evasive, but for the best of reasons. At six this evening, all will be revealed. Can you trust me until then?"

"You know I trust you with my life," his voice grated.

With those words she jumped out of the car and hurried inside first. When he followed her through the door, he had to run to catch up with her. She reached the bedroom first. "I thought you'd never get here."

"Mignonne—" He caught her to him. The moment their mouths fused in need, the world reeled. His loving took her to such a divine place, she almost forgot about the party.

"Darling? What time is it?"

"Ten to six."

"Uh-oh. We have to get ready."

"For what?"

"You'll find out. Put on something semi-dressy. I'll shower first." She dashed away before he could pull her back. They were going to be late.

At ten after six she walked in the living room where he was waiting for her. As Josette had predicted, his black eyes glittered with desire as he studied every curving inch of her. "I approve of your shopping spree."

"Good. I like your black silky shirt. You're

impossibly handsome, you know. So handsome, I'd like to lock myself up in a tower with you."

She thought he sounded a little out of breath. "Where are we going?"

"To the château."

He looked taken aback. "I don't understand."

"You will. In fact you're going to have to show me where to go. We were due at your parents' suite ten minutes ago."

Raoul shook his head. "Don't tease me about this."

"I'm not, my darling." She grabbed the sack with the presents. "We need to hurry."

Abby started for the car first and got in without his help. He was totally quiet as he drove them to another entrance to the château she hadn't seen before. This time he opened the car door for her. Before he let her go, he ran his hands over her hips and back. "You're so beautiful, it hurts."

She kissed his lips before hurrying inside with him. He led her up the stairs to the second floor. When they came to the entrance, the doors had been opened. Abby hooked her arm through his and they walked inside.

The first person they saw was an adorable brunette boy who came running toward Raoul, calling out something like "Rool." Abby loved the little guy already. Her husband picked him up in his arms.

Maurice asked him something in French. "What he did say, Rool?"

Raoul's laughter delighted her. "He wanted to know if I bought him a present while I was in Paris. I can't believe it, but I forgot to get him anything on this trip."

"No, you didn't." She lifted the sack. "These are for him."

His black eyes stared at her in shock.

"Go on. Give them to him."

He carried Maurice to the couch in the salon and reached inside the bag to hand him his presents. Josette and Paul came in to see what was going on. A smile lit up their faces to watch as their boy tore off the wrapping paper and examined his new toys.

Raoul grabbed Abby around the waist, propelled by emotions erupting inside of him. He stared at his sister. "You look lovely tonight."

"Don't they both?" Paul had his arm around her shoulders. "Our wives went on a shopping spree while we were away. I have a feeling we're in for it when we have to travel on business."

Abby shook her head. "*Mon mari* won't be leaving town any time soon, so you don't need to worry."

Josette smiled. "Maman has dinner waiting for us on the *terrasse*."

Once again Raoul stared at Abby. She grasped his hand. "Come on."

Paul swept Maurice into his arms, toys and all, and they walked through the suite to the *terrasse* that overlooked a fabulous rose garden. Abby heard one of those male whistles and looked to the side. Jean-Marc stood there with his arms folded, wearing a grin.

"Congratulations on your marriage." He walked toward her and kissed her on both cheeks. "I should have been the one who went to Switzerland." Then he faced his brother and gave him a hug that brought tears to her eyes.

Over their shoulders she saw his mother wheel their father over to them. She wore a filmy yellow dress. On the shoulder, she was wearing the pin. Abby could hardly breathe.

"We're so happy for the two you." She approached Raoul who wrapped his arms around her. As they clung, his father eyed Abby. "My son is a very fortunate man. If you'd lean over, I'd like to give you a kiss and welcome you to the family."

Abby's heart was full to overflowing as she did his bidding. They kissed on both cheeks. He was probably in pain to put forth that much exertion. But the fact that he made the effort meant the world to her.

Raoul watched the two of them as if he couldn't believe what he was seeing. His father finally looked at her husband. Abby saw love in those dark eyes before he held up his

278 CAPTIVATED BY THE BROODING BILLIONAIRE

hands. The sight of father and son embracing would be etched in her mind and heart forever.

Paul had put Maurice in a high chair. He kept tapping his kaleidoscope against the tray. Abby hurried around and sat down to talk to him. "Will you let me show you?" Of course, he didn't understand her. She put it to her eye, then urged him to do the same.

Josette said something to him in French and suddenly Abby could tell he was seeing the designs inside.

"I'm starting French lessons and can't wait until I can talk to him."

"He'll love it, but I'm afraid I'm going to have to put him to bed in a minute."

"Thank you for letting him stay up."

Raoul sat down next to Abby and put his hand on her thigh beneath the table. Heat rushed to her face. She couldn't look at him as everyone gathered and their meal was served.

His mother looked at Abby. "This is such a special occasion, I cooked dinner myself. This was always Raoul's favorite. Rack of lamb and mint from our garden. Before we eat, I'd like to make a toast to our son and his bride." She lifted her glass. "To new beginnings."

Abby knew they were drinking the most treasured pinot noir from their vaunted wine cellar. After she swallowed a healthy amount, Jean-Marc raised his glass. "Here's to the fresh California breeze that has blown through the vineyard."

"Amen," Paul chimed in.

"That was very poetic for you," Josette teased her younger brother and held up her glass. "To a new friend I like very much."

Their father kept his hand around his glass, but Abby knew he was going to say something. "This is good. To my family."

Raoul had to be overcome. She waited while he cleared his throat. Then he stood up with his glass. "As you all can see, with Abby in my life... I've been reborn." He kept swallowing. "Thank you," he whispered.

Please, please, let this last, Abby prayed while they ate together, amused by Maurice's antics.

Toward the end of the meal his mother stood up. "We'll have dessert with the grandparents now. It's your favorite, Raoul, my *crème brûlée*."

Raoul clung to Abby's hand. She knew he was still in disbelief that any of this was happening. She could hardly believe it herself. They moved as a group to the other end of the second floor and gathered around the salon with the grandparents.

"This is divine, Hélène-Claire. I want the recipes for everything you've made tonight. A wife wants to be everything to her husband, but there's no way she can compete with his mother's cooking."

Raoul's grandmother nodded. "You are very wise for one so young."

Josette broke in on them. "I've got to get Maurice to bed." She eyed Abby. "We'll talk soon."

"Please."

"It's time for us to leave too." Raoul got up to kiss his grandparents and parents.

Abby turned to everyone. "This has been one of the most wonderful evenings of my life."

His mother followed them to the entrance of the suite. "We'll do it again with the entire family after your church wedding. Let us know when you want to plan it."

"Merci, Maman."

He whisked Abby down the hall to the other end of the château where the car was parked outside. Silence reigned during the drive back to the cottage. She found herself savoring this night. When he took her inside their house, she grasped both his hands and kissed them.

"Your heart has to be so full. After we get in bed, I'll tell you what happened after you left for Paris. I thought it was a miracle. Tonight, I know it was. I really like your family. All of them. Because they love you, they're trying to like me. I can't ask for more than that as long as you love me."

"Jean-Marc said it best. You *are* the fresh breeze blowing through the vineyard, casting a spell on everyone, including your husband who adores you." He picked her up and carried her into the bedroom. "Get ready to be loved tonight like you've never been loved before."

EPILOGUE

FAR INTO THE night Raoul came awake and reached for Abby. Since their marriage four months ago he still awoke with anxiety at times, in case this was all a dream and she wasn't really there.

"Mon amour," he whispered, rubbing her arm gently until she turned to him.

"Raoul—" His loving wife gave him a kiss of such desire, he was breathless as they lost themselves in each other for the next few hours. He'd never dreamed marriage could be like this. He hadn't thought it possible. "No man could be as happy as I am."

"I hope that's true," she spoke against his lips. "But to make certain of it, I have a gift for you I know you're going to love."

"Is that so?"

"Yes."

"Are you going to give it to me now?"

"Not quite yet."

He raised up on one elbow. "That's not fair."

"I know, but I love teasing you."

Raoul kissed her throat. "Give me a hint. Is it expensive?"

"I don't know yet."

"What do you mean?"

"We'll have to wait and see after it arrives."

"Did you buy it in Dijon?"

"No. It's coming from an entirely different place."

"Abby—" He rolled her on top of him. "You're being very playful tonight. What's going on?"

She covered his face with kisses. "It just so happens that no woman could be as happy as I am tonight. After my French tutoring session in town this morning, I made one more stop before coming home and found out I'm *enceinte*. Did I pronounce it right?"

"You're *what*?"

"I thought that might get your attention. Dr. Filbert says we won't be able to tell the sex of our *bébé* for a little while longer, but we're definitely expecting. I was going to tell you in the morning, but since you woke me up now, I decided I couldn't keep it a secret any longer."

She felt him tremble with excitement. He rolled her carefully on to her side. After feeling her stomach, he leaned down and kissed the place where it was growing. When he lifted his head to kiss her, he tasted the salt from her tears.

"Isn't it wonderful, Raoul? You're going to be able to raise your second child and you'll be the most wonderful father in the world."

Tears sprang to his eyes. He embraced her gently. "I was just going to say what a beautiful mother you're going to make. I'm the luckiest husband alive."

"I only have one request. I would like you to choose the name if we have a boy. But if it's a girl, I want to call her Blondine. Won't it be thrilling for her to read the storybook her *papa* loved?"

"*Abby—*"

* * * * *

LET'S TALK

Romance

For exclusive extracts, competitions
and special offers, find us online:

Or get in touch on 0844 844 1351*

For all the latest titles coming soon,
visit millsandboon.co.uk/nextmonth

Want even more
ROMANCE?

Join our bookclub today!

'Mills & Boon books, the perfect way to escape for an hour or so.'

Miss W. Dyer

'Excellent service, promptly delivered and very good subscription choices.'

Miss A. Pearson

'You get fantastic special offers and the chance to get books before they hit the shops'

Mrs V. Hall

Visit millsandbook.co.uk/Bookclub and save on brand new books.

MILLS & BOON